LIGHTS, CAMERA, LOVE

Holly flopped down on her bed and pulled
out her script for next week's TV episode of "Hartley Square." She flipped
through the pages until she found her
part. There it was—LINDSEY, *Scene 3B
. . . Backstage at local disco.* Holly began to read and then did a double take.
JED, *catching* LINDSEY *off guard, tilts her
chin up and kisses her.*

Holly was stunned. Her first television
kiss—no, her first kiss, period—and nobody had seen fit to tell her, not even the
director. Holly tried to imagine kissing the
actor who played Jed, but just couldn't.

Now, if it were Tim . . .

Lights, Camera, Love

Gailanne Maravel

BANTAM BOOKS
TORONTO · NEW YORK · LONDON · SYDNEY

RL 5, IL age 11 and up

LIGHTS, CAMERA, LOVE
A Bantam Book / November 1983

Cover photo by Pat Hill

ISBN 0-553-23746-2

Published simultaneously in the United States and Canada

Bantam Books are published by Bantam Books, Inc. Its trademark,
consisting of the words ''Bantam Books'' and the portrayal of a
rooster, is Registered in U.S. Patent and Trademark Office and in
other countries. Marca Registrada. Bantam Books, Inc., 666 Fifth
Avenue, New York, New York 10103.

PRINTED IN THE UNITED STATES OF AMERICA

O   0 9 8 7 6 5 4 3 2 1

For Sheila—teacher
and forever friend

The author acknowledges the cast and
crew of the CBS serial "The Guiding
Light," especially Jennifer Cooke and Ed
Devlin.

Chapter One

That week Lindsey would have to face her kidnappers in court. The prosecutor would ask her to point out the pair who had held her captive in the isolated mountain cabin for a week. "That's them. Over there!" And she would point in the direction of the defendants' table. But how should she deliver those lines? Should it be with fear in her voice, shyness, or brave boldness?

Holly Giles felt the bus jolt as it hit a pothole. She put the script she was studying in her lap. "That's them. Over there!" she repeated to herself. Holly decided that Lindsey, the character she portrayed on TV's leading soap opera, "Hartley Square," would cry the line out, collapse on the witness stand, and be led away, sobbing, by her anxious parents and the handsome young prosecutor. Unless the director had other ideas, of course. But he usually told her to trust her instincts, and Holly's instincts concerning the character of Lindsey were seldom wrong.

The bus carrying residents back from the beach to the town of Amsbly inched along Shore Road in second gear, and Holly geared her stomach for every familiar bump. Running her fingers through her short, light brown hair, still damp from swimming, she glanced over at her friend Andrea Gelfand, seated next to her. Andrea and the book she was reading bobbed in rhythm to the jerky movements of the bus. Holly smiled, wondering if the next jolt would send the book flying.

"Read something for me and tell me how you think Lindsey would deliver this line." Holly snatched Andrea's book out of her hands and passed the script to her.

Andrea sighed in mock annoyance. "It's almost impossible to read anything on this bus. It would be easier on a toboggan run!" But she obligingly scanned the page Holly indicated. After a few minutes she said, "Now I don't have to watch you on HS next week."

"Why not?"

"Well, you've already been rescued from the kidnappers, and obviously your father has pressed for an early court date. Not that I ever doubted you'd be saved by the cute ranger in the cabin. . . ." Her voice trailed off as she continued to read.

"That transparent, huh?" Holly laughed, remembering the many jokes they had shared about the convoluted plots of daytime drama.

"No, not really," Andrea said. "I knew you'd be rescued—otherwise you'd have told me they were cutting you out of the show. But you were playing those cabin scenes so well, I thought they'd drag it out a little longer."

"Thanks for the kind words. I'd take a bow, but we're approaching the Pier Street ruts, and I'd fall out of my seat!"

Although Holly had responded lightly, she was grateful for Andrea's praise. Aside from her own parents, no one but Andrea ever admitted watching her on the show. Holly wondered, as she had many times before, why she had made so few friends when she was in junior high. She supposed some of it was her own fault. Ever since she'd been cast in "Hartley Square" at the beginning of seventh grade, there just hadn't been enough time to participate in school activities. She couldn't even try out for cheerleading, which had cut her off from the most popular girls in school. Many of them were jealous of Holly's

3

new career, she knew, especially since she'd gotten the opportunity to audition for the part because her godfather was an associate producer of the show.

If I'd only had the time to let them get to know me better, they would have known that there was no reason to be jealous, Holly thought. I had to work as hard as anyone else to get that role.

Holly also had a sneaking suspicion that the kids in her ninth-grade class had tended to confuse Holly Giles with the character she played on "Hartley Square." Wealthy, spoiled Lindsey Amies was a far cry from the person Holly was, but her acting ability made it seem that Lindsey and Holly were two sides of the same coin.

Boys in her junior high had been another problem altogether. The ones she might have liked were reluctant to approach her— maybe they were afraid of being turned down by a "star." Others had come on strong, thinking she was more sophisticated than the other girls, both because of the character she played and because she was an actress. Holly had completed junior high with a perfect record— she had never had one date! She hoped that high school was going to be different.

"She'd play it for all it's worth," Andrea

said, interrupting Holly's thoughts, and tossed the script back into her lap.

"What?"

"You're daydreaming again. I was talking about Lindsey's courtroom scene. She'd cry, scream—anything to bring her divorced parents rushing to her side. She's pulled every trick in the book to get her parents back together since her stepfather's death."

"You're right, as usual," said Holly ruefully. "Ever think of becoming a director?"

They were sitting in one of the long rows, and Andrea was looking out the window as the bus came to a stop. Suddenly she stiffened. Then she moved her beach bag off the seat to her right and slid into the empty seat. "Yeah— I'm going to direct you right now. Slide to your right!"

"Huh?"

"Now! Move! *He's* getting on the bus at Bay Street. If you slide over next to me, the only empty space will be next to you." She was speaking hurriedly and pulling Holly at the same time.

"Who's 'he'?" Holly asked as she followed her friend's instructions.

"Tim," Andrea said with some annoyance. "The boy who works at White's Grocery. The one you always stare at when you drag me into the store on all kinds of ridiculous errands."

"They aren't ridiculous. I have to go to the store a lot for my mother—and I *haven't* been staring! Really, I'm not that obvious—am I?" The last remark made Andrea giggle.

"The other day you bought an *avocado*. I mean, I could have died laughing. You hate avocados. Here he comes." Andrea's voice had dropped to a whisper, and she buried her nose in her book, but her large brown eyes peered above the pages, checking out the newest arrival.

The bus lurched forward, and Tim fell against Holly's shoulder as he slid into the seat next to her.

"I'm sorry," he said, smiling. Holly took in every detail—from his blue running shoes to his light auburn hair.

"It's OK. It's first gear," she said. Tim looked puzzled. She explained, "You have to hold on somewhere and not try for a seat until he gets the bus into second. I've been riding this bus for years."

Tim laughed. "I'll remember that."

Holly smiled and looked down at her beach bag. "Your foot seems to be caught in the handle of my bag."

For an instant he seemed flustered, but

then he grinned. "First I fall on you, and then I get tangled up in your beach bag. Very uncool," he said apologetically.

As he reached down to slide the bag off his foot, his hand lightly brushed Holly's arm. She felt her face color and glanced at Andrea, who winked, then went back to her book.

"I've seen you in the grocery store a lot," Tim continued. "You're Holly, right?"

"Yes. And I know you're Tim. I heard your boss call you one day. I *do* go to the store a lot—to help my mother. She's always forgetting things." Holly took a deep swallow before her last sentence. She also felt Andrea's elbow dig her in her ribs.

Tim didn't see the look Holly shot at Andrea. "I knew who you were even before I saw you in the store. Someone pointed you out. You're in the theater or something, aren't you?"

"Television," Andrea supplied. It was the first time Tim was aware of her presence. Holly introduced them, and Andrea replied sweetly, "Don't pay any attention to me. I'm reading my book."

"Right. Television. It's a program called . . ." Tim pushed the hair from his forehead as if hoping the name of the program would flash before his eyes.

7

" 'Hartley Square,' or HS as we call it."
Holly looked for some sign of recognition from
him and saw none. "It's a soap opera. I just
have a small part."

"Oh, sure! One of the cashiers turns it
on every day in the back. She takes her break
just to watch it. I guess I've just been too
busy to watch. Now I really feel dumb."

"Don't," Holly said quickly. She thought
for a moment, then added, "In fact, it's kind
of nice to meet someone who doesn't come on
to me because they think I'm glamorous—
which I'm not—or a star—which I'm also not!"

"Thanks for saying that. You make a person feel very comfortable, you know?" Tim
paused. "You don't go to Amsbly High, do
you? I know I haven't seen you there—I'd
remember if I had." He looked straight into
her brown eyes as he spoke. Holly, flustered,
bent over and reached for her beach bag,
tossing in the script.

"I'm starting at Haycroft Academy, the
girls' school, in September. Actually, that's a
few days. So will Andrea," she told him, indicating her friend, still apparently absorbed in
her book.

"That's too bad." Tim sounded disappointed. Then his face brightened. "But I'll be seeing
you in the store, won't I?"

"You sure will," Holly assured him warmly. "Oh, here's our stop." Holly and Andrea scrambled for their bags and stood up.

"It was nice talking to you," Holly added, feeling suddenly shy.

"You too, Holly—and Andrea." Andrea smiled and said nothing.

Holly descended the steps of the bus, waiting for the door to give its familiar hiss before opening.

"Hey, Holly!" Tim called. "I forgot to ask you your last name."

"Giles." She was almost out the door but turned back. "What's yours?"

"Hartley," he returned, with a perfectly straight face. The door snapped shut, leaving Holly and Andrea on the curb, staring after the departing bus.

The girls stared at each other in surprise. "Talk about coincidence!" Andrea said, whooping.

"I think it's great! Now I *really* like him," said Holly, joyfully swinging her beach bag in a circle around her.

"That much I knew from the way you looked at him in the store," Andrea said dryly.

"That was different. Then I just liked the way he *looked*; he's really handsome. But now I like him as a person." Holly was glowing.

"He's A-number-one genuine. And you know what? I think he likes me. Oh, Andrea!"

"Oh, brother. I can deal with Lindsey's emotionalism, but this is too much to take!" Andrea made a pretense of fainting, and Holly swatted her with her script.

They stood watching the bus crawl toward town, leaving in its wake a cloud of black smoke. Holly was thinking of Tim still sitting there, probably laughing to himself.

"That bus is hazardous to health," Andrea quipped. "Are you coming, Miss Dreamy Eyes, or am I walking alone?"

Holly let out a sigh as she caught up with her friend, who was already several yards ahead of her. "You know, Andrea, my father says that's the same bus he rode when he was a teenager. Can you imagine what it must have been like then when there was no Sea Gull Lane or Surf Road—just miles of dunes with fishing shacks tucked in between? I'll bet it was really isolated and beautiful in a mysterious sort of way."

"You're sounding weird. That's a symptom, Holly."

"Of what?"

"Lovesickness!" Andrea recoiled to avoid Holly's playful punch.

"Where's your sense of romance?" Holly snapped as they neared her house.

"Speaking of romance, what's going on with Kim at HS?" Andrea asked, to change the subject. "Is she going to have her baby? It seems like a year already."

"You're supposed to tune in and find out," Holly said, teasing, then relented. "OK, I'll fill you in. Kim's going to have to keep padding her wardrobe with pillows. Her husband is away at a medical convention. Actually, the guy who *plays* her husband is touring with a summer stock job, so as soon as he gets back, he'll rush to the hospital in time for the birth."

"Finally!" Andrea laughed, clutching her stomach. "I feel like an anxious aunt-to-be. What about Lindsey? I mean, after next week's court scene."

"I think I'm going to find a boyfriend." Holly had a faraway look in her eyes.

"You mean *Lindsey*, don't you?"

"You figure it out," Holly said with a dramatic flourish. "Call you tomorrow," she added as she sprinted up the steps to her front door.

The instant she went inside, Holly was hit by the fumes of the charcoal starter her father was using on the patio. Each time

11

they cooked out, her mother would remind him to keep the patio doors shut, and each time he'd forget. Holly put down her things and started the salad—her longtime family job. She could see her father bending over the barbecue and fanning the coals. Holly smiled, anticipating the next words to be spoken when her mother came down the stairs.

She was right.

"Jeff! How many times have I asked you to keep those doors closed? You should smell this house! If I struck a match, we'd all blow up!" Holly's mother slid the patio doors closed and gave Holly her "it's hopeless" shrug.

"Holly, you look flushed," her mother continued. "Did you get too much sun today?" Mrs. Giles kissed her and touched her daughter's pink cheek.

"I'm fine. The color will fade by tomorrow—it always does."

Even this had become a familiar line to Holly. But she didn't mind the routine or the questions. In fact, she often felt she needed them to balance the unreal world of her television life.

As Holly sliced the tomatoes, fresh from her mother's garden, she thought back to the bus ride and Tim, remembering how shy she'd felt just before she'd gotten off. Funny—she was an actress who could do anything in front of a camera, but in real life . . .

I'm Holly, not Lindsey, she said to herself. Maybe Lindsey would be able to handle meeting a boy she really liked and hadn't spoken to before, but she'd have a script to guide her. And I'm not Lindsey. Holly peeled an avocado, then popped a piece into her mouth and made a face. It's got to be an acquired taste, she said to herself. I'll bet Lindsey likes avocados!

Chapter Two

EPISODE #4,937

HARTLEY SQUARE
ACT V: SCENE 7A

[Courtroom: Late Morning. Sunlight streaming through windows. JUDGE, JURORS, SPECTATORS ASSEMBLED. LINDSEY, looking apprehensive, is in witness box. SPECTATORS murmuring. Then silence as prosecutor PAUL WOLFE approaches Lindsey.]

PAUL: Now, Lindsey—there, there. We all know the ordeal you have been through. I have only one more question to ask you. Will you tell the court if the two persons who kidnapped you are present in the courtroom? *[LINDSEY nods, eyes downcast]* Let the record show that the witness has indicated in the affirmative. Now, Lindsey, would you point them out for the court?

LINDSEY: [*hand trembling, points.*] That's them. Over there. [LINDSEY, *sobbing, collapses in tears.*]

PAUL: Your Honor, I request a recess. The witness is clearly distraught.

JUDGE COOPER: Permission granted. This court will recess until two PM.

BAILIFF: All rise. [JUDGE, JURORS *exit. Spectator background noise.* PARENTS *rush to Lindsey.* PAUL *puts arm around her, leading her down from stand.* LINDSEY *faces kidnappers once more. Take* LINDSEY. *Fade. Cue commercial:* Desert-Dri Deodorant.]

"Cut. Kill floor mike." Holly heard the familiar end to a taping, turned off Lindsey's hysterics, and straightened up to smile at her TV parents.

Van Tyler, who played the prosecutor, took his arm from Holly's shoulders and gave her a pat on the head. "You were great, kiddo. I hope I didn't throw you too much, putting in that bit about offering you a cup of water. It just seemed right for the moment, and I think it worked."

"You bet it worked, but in the future, keep the surprises to a minimum." Director Chris Costas had approached them. "Holly, you're a natural. That last take of you looking at the kidnappers was perfect."

"Thanks, Chris. And, Van, I hope we do another scene together sometime. It was fun."

"Who knows"—he winked at her—"we may wind up married someday—a May-December romance."

"You're insane," she said, laughing, and waved him away. She walked from the set, carefully stepping over the miles of cables snaked around the barnlike studio. To her right was a mock-up of an airplane cockpit. To her left, lighting technicians were testing for the next set. Holly was finished for the day but in no hurry to get to her dressing room. The dress that the wardrobe department had selected for her was one she wished she owned. Holly liked the feel of the navy blue silk against her skin.

"Hey, Holly! You in this one, or just watching?" It was the technician everyone called Grandpa.

"No, Grandpa. Just watching." She smiled as he turned his light meter toward the set of a townhouse bedroom. After three years of acting on the soap, Holly felt that he and the rest of the cast and crew were like an extended family. The set she most enjoyed was her TV family's living room. It was not at all like her own at home. This make-believe room was filled with peach-cushioned furniture, modern art, and lots of glimmering chrome. Her own home was definitely more comfortable, she decided, if not as dazzling.

Home. Holly knew she'd better get moving if she wanted to make the 4:34 train from Penn Station to Amsbly. Heading for her dressing room, she greeted cast members who had been paged for the next scene. The hallway to the dressing room wing held still more of the cast, some in bathrobes waiting to go into makeup. All in all, Holly thought, it looked like her idea of a campus dorm, and she was glad about that. There were no silver stars on the doors.

"Hi, Billy." Holly poked her head in the door next to hers. Billy Gabriel, who played up-and-coming rock star Jed Shine on the show, was sitting cross-legged on the floor, guitar in hand.

"How's it going, Holly? Got time to hear a new song I'm doing on the show next week?"

"Sorry, Billy, I'll have to wait until next week. I've got a train to catch." She stepped back into the hallway and heard the sounds of Billy strumming and singing, "Farewell, Holly. Off to Amsbly. Clickity-clack, train's on the track."

"Oh, terrific," she hollered. "That's bound to get you a gold record."

Her script for the following week's segment was on the dressing table. Holly glanced at the top blue sheet to see which studio she'd be shooting in and started to remove her makeup. "Yuk," she said as she wiped off the last of the orange foundation. On TV the makeup looked perfect. In natural light she felt clownlike and couldn't wait to wash off the mask. Door closed, Holly slipped off the blue silk and gave it one longing look. She pulled on her jeans, thinking they felt rough after the delicate fabric.

After she was dressed, she threw the script in her canvas bag, then headed for the lobby. "Bye, Terry, see you next week," she called to the security guard at the main entrance.

"Won't be seeing too much of you with school starting, I guess," he said. He added, "Watch out—lot of fans out there."

Outside she signed a few autographs while keeping an eye peeled for a taxi. When one appeared, she signaled and made her apologies to the soap fans. "I'm really sorry," she said sincerely, "but I've got a train to catch."

"Hey, you somebody important?" the cab-driver asked, looking in his rearview mirror.

"No, Nobody important," she said cheerfully and settled back into the seat.

Holly called it the road to and from "Hartley Square": it was the route the train took from the suburb of Amsbly to Manhattan and back again. She had long ago memorized every landmark along the way. Before reaching for her new script to study, she counted the number of times the automated pot on the billboard for Williamson's Coffee tipped and poured before it was all whisked from her view. Commuting was a matter of fact, as much a part of her life as going to school.

School! Holly could hardly believe she would be entering Haycroft Academy in a few days. Maybe a new start was just what she needed. She'd make more time to get to know the other girls, and they would get to understand that she was just a regular kid, even if she had a career. Meeting Tim the previous day seemed a turning point. If I start thinking about Tim now, I'll never look at next week's script, she said to herself.

"Enough!" Holly said out loud without realizing it. The woman sitting next to her jumped. Holly managed a smile, hoping the woman wouldn't think she was losing her mind. She started leafing through the bulky script. It was important for her to go over all the scenes whether or not she was in them. Any new twist in the plot might affect the way Holly played her own scenes. Besides, she was just as curious as the average viewer as to what was going to happen next on HS. She learned, for example, that Aunt Lydia, the head of the family and the family's cosmetics industry, had rushed back to her townhouse from her summer seaside compound.

"Hmm. What's bringing her back so early?" Holly realized it was the woman next to her who was speaking and reading along with her. "Oh, don't mind me, dear. You know, it wasn't until you spoke that I realized who you were. I'm a longtime fan of "Hartley Square," and you're little Lindsey!" She spoke like an adoring grandmother, and Holly couldn't help but like her.

"I'm glad you enjoy the program."

"Oh my, yes! I can't say I see eye to eye with Lydia all the time, but I suppose a family as large and spread out as hers needs a figurehead. It's when she gets on that high horse of hers and starts running people's lives—well! I hope you're not going to let her do that to you, dear."

Holly could hardly keep from laughing. The woman was so genuine and so involved with the characters. "I don't know for sure, but I *do* know Lydia has called my parents to her parlor and ordered them to put an end to the publicity about the family now that the kidnapping has been solved."

"Oh, she's got other motives, I'm sure of that. But it's time that you got on with your life after all you've been through." The woman really seemed to think she was talking to Lindsey.

Holly kept up the conversation for the woman's sake and found herself enjoying the experience. "My mother is going to persuade my cousin Sheila to take me to a rock concert with her, to get me back into the mainstream."

"Humph! 'Persuade' is right! That little flirt, Sheila! She's jealous of all the attention you get. She's got a crush on that rock star, you know, and she'll probably be worried that you'll steal him away, you being so pretty and all."

"Thank you," Holly said, hoping the compliment was meant for her as well as Lindsey.

"Well, dear, I get off at the next stop. Now you take my advice. Keep trying to bring your parents back together. Families—the backbone of this nation. And watch out for that singer fellow—too smooth—could be trouble for you. Find yourself a nice boy." The train glided to a stop as the woman rose. "See you Monday afternoon," she said in a chirpy voice and waved a white glove at Holly.

Holly thought she'd burst. Wait until she told the other actors about the woman on the train! It was hard to get back to the script and concentrate on finding her scene.

There it was: SCENE 3B . . . Dry rehearsal at 7 AM . . . LINDSEY, JED, SHEILA, JED'S MANAGER, EXTRAS. Holly flipped to page fifty-two. *Backstage at local disco.* Holly began to read, then did a double take. JED, *catching Lindsey off guard, takes her chin and kisses her.* LINDSEY *enjoying kiss but backs off, stunned.*

Stunned wasn't the word for it. Holly was outraged. Had Billy known about this today? she wondered. Chris hadn't said anything about it, and he was the director. Lindsey's first television kiss, and nobody had seen fit to tell her about it! Holly tried to imagine kissing Billy but just couldn't picture it. Now if it were Tim . . .

But it wasn't.

She arrived home angry, taking her frustration out on the front door.

"Holly, please," Mrs. Giles said as she came to greet her daughter. "That door has been around for twenty-some years, and if you'd treat it more kindly, it could last another fifty."

"You have no idea how annoyed I am!" Holly dropped into the blue velvet chair near the fireplace. "This is one script that's got to be rewritten!"

"Calm down, dear. This isn't like you at all. You've always loved what you were doing, which is why we've agreed to let you continue on the show. A fit of temperament doesn't suit you." Mrs. Giles sat down opposite Holly.

"I'm calm now that I'm home. Just let me think about this for a while—the script, I mean—and then if I need to, I'll talk to you and Dad about the problem."

"That's fine with me. I'm going to make us some lemonade," Mrs. Giles said, getting up and smoothing her skirt. "Oh, by the way, you had a call—but it may be some sort of prank. It was a boy—claimed his name was Hartley. He said he'd call back. Maybe you'd better let your father or me answer the phone tonight."

Holly rocketed from her chair. "*Hartley!* That's Tim, a boy I've sort of met—know. It's not a joke. Really! that's his name."

"Well, I must say you look like yourself again. Hartley," Mrs. Giles mused as she left the room. "What a coincidence."

Holly felt all her earlier irritation leaving. Tim, she thought, sighing happily as she sank back into the wing chair. If I'm lucky, she thought, maybe I'll beat Lindsey to having *her* first kiss!

Chapter Three

When the phone rang later that evening, Holly picked up the receiver eagerly and was delighted to hear Tim's voice.

"Just thought it was time for a Hartley-to-Hartley talk," Tim joked, and Holly groaned appreciatively. "I didn't plan what happened on the bus that day. I was going to tell you up front what my last name was, but it didn't work out that way," he continued.

"I'm beginning to understand your sense of humor," said Holly. "It certainly was an original approach—claiming to be named Hartley."

"Claiming? That is my name," Tim said indignantly.

"I know," Holly said soothingly. "Just kidding."

"OK, score one for you. You know, when the bus pulled away the other day, I thought maybe I'd blown my chance of getting to know you better—that maybe you'd think I was putting you on, and you'd be angry."

"No, I'm not angry," Holly assured him.

"Great!" He waited for her to say something further, and when she didn't, added, "I mean, I thought, maybe you have a boyfriend or something—"

"No, I don't have a boyfriend, and I'd like to know you better, too." Holly had never dreamed she'd be saying those words to Tim, but it felt perfectly right.

Tim resumed the conversation after a sigh of evident relief. "I was hoping you'd say that. I wanted to ask to see you again, and when I called, I was going to say something cool like, 'How about a night at the opera or a day at the soap?' but it's not my style. Maybe it's not yours, either."

"It's not," she admitted, then started to laugh. "But I appreciate the thought."

"If you could stop laughing long enough, we could figure out when we could meet. I've got to work until nine tomorrow night, Sunday's my mother's birthday, and I've already got plans for Labor Day. So how about Tuesday after school?"

"Don't you work Tuesday?" Holly asked.

"Not till four-thirty. I could get over to Haycroft by three-twenty, and maybe we could just walk or stop for a soda. How does that sound?"

Holly gulped. "It sounds fine!"

"Then I'll see you at the hallowed halls of Haycroft on Tuesday."

"OK. See you then."

Holly carefully replaced the receiver and then let out a shriek. "WHOOPEE!" She just barely held back from doing a cartwheel across the living room floor.

"Holly, honestly!" Mrs. Giles was wearing her stern look, but Mr. Giles winked. "You're screaming loud enough to wake the dead."

"Sorry, Mom," Holly replied, but she definitely didn't feel sorry. Her smile was the one she used when Lindsey was happy, but that night it was all her own. A date! Her very first date!

A new school, and just maybe a new beginning, Holly hoped, as she walked alone to Haycroft on Tuesday morning. It will be different this year, I can feel it, she said to herself. I'll make new friends, and there will be dances and parties—everything I've missed out on. She took a deep breath and began

27

climbing the hill toward the school. She remembered with amusement that there had been a time when the mere sight of the formidable old buildings had made the hairs on the back of her neck stand on end. But that was when she had been very young.

Holly and her parents had been driving home on a snowy night. She had been asleep in the backseat, and when she woke up, the car was moving slowly along the road past Haycroft. Her first sight from the car window had been of the huge old oak trees, their bare branches reaching toward the moon like twisted fingers. And when she had seen the series of night lights in the stone buildings, it had seemed to her that they formed the outline of a frightening, howling face. She had shivered, and for many years afterward had felt uncomfortable each time she passed the school.

But on that bright September day, Holly thought it looked anything but ominous, and she smiled at her childish fears. She felt much too optimistic to let any dark thoughts cloud her mood.

She was looking forward to meeting Tim after school, but she did miss sharing her first day with Andrea. Andrea's mother had insisted on escorting her daughter on her first day at Haycroft. "It's all too juvenile for words," Andrea had said, "but since the divorce, my mother's been out for the title of Super Mom."

Holly mounted the century-old stone steps to the main building, trailing a bevy of girls in designer jeans and miniskirts. There was no dress code at Haycroft, and Holly was glad that she'd decided to wear her new designer jeans and Izod shirt. She *looked* the part—surely they'd accept her.

It wasn't until the break between homeroom and first period that Holly and Andrea were able to compare schedules and find they were in only two classes together—PE and geometry. Holly was disappointed.

"The school is so small. I thought we'd have almost the same schedule. But I guess I should have expected it," she said ruefully. "My schedule had to be worked out with free periods some mornings so that I could do the soap without missing classes."

"Don't worry about it," Andrea said. "You'll meet kids you like in no time. I did in homeroom. I'll save a seat for you at lunch and introduce you. We'd better run, or we'll be late."

29

For one split second Holly felt a twinge of envy. Andrea never seemed to have a problem making friends, even in a brand new school. Before she could dwell on that thought, a bell sounded, and Holly ran off to find biology in Room 142.

The dining hall was just that—not a cafeteria like the one she'd been used to in junior high, but an oak-paneled room complete with pastoral murals. Even the chairs and tables were not the usual plastic-and-chrome public school issue. There were dark polished wooden tables with ladder-back chairs, and they all seemed to be occupied by a hundred or more strangers. Holly surveyed the scene while waiting for her tray to be filled.

"Holly, over here!" Thank heavens for Andrea, Holly thought as she weaved her way through tables to where her friend was sitting.

Andrea pulled out the chair she had reserved for Holly. "Hi! How was your morning? No, wait. Tell me later. I want you to meet some of the girls in my homeroom. They've all known each other forever, so you and I are the only new ones at the table."

The names came at her much too fast, and they all sounded alike. "Holly, meet

Amanda, Samantha, Miranda, Hailey, and Carley."

Holly wished for a replay but instead gave a general "hi" and sat down.

Say something, Holly said to herself. You don't want them to think you're stuck-up, or you'll end up an outsider like you were before. She smiled nervously and said aloud, "I think it's great that you were all lucky enough to be in the same homeroom." She was met with silence.

Finally someone spoke. Holly thought it was Amanda. "It's not luck. It's a matter of whose parents know the headmistress." Amanda was the one with the poppy red hair and matching lipstick.

Another girl said, "Being a famous TV star won't get you special treatment at Haycroft."

No way I'm going to let that remark stand, Holly thought, raging inside. "First of all, I'm not a star. Second, I haven't asked for any favors. I'm looking forward to being just a regular student." Her voice trembled with anger and disappointment. The other girls exchanged glances, then started giggling and talking about people and events that Holly had never heard of, pointedly ignoring Holly and Andrea. Holly's throat felt tight and dry, and she could hardly swallow her lukewarm chili. Why couldn't life be like a TV script, all worked out in advance so you could flip through the pages and find out what was going to happen next? At least then she'd be prepared. This scenario wasn't at all the way she had imagined it.

"You didn't have to come down on them so hard," Andrea whispered as they filed out of the dining hall.

"Hard on *them!* Whose side are you on, anyway?" Holly snapped, bewildered by Andrea's reaction.

"Well, give them a chance. Don't write them off the first day. And calm down."

"When is someone going to give *me* a chance?" Holly almost cried but blinked back her tears. Her voice softened. "I'm sorry I yelled at you. It's just that I wanted everything to go perfectly today. I was sure I was going to make friends and feel a part of things at last."

"It can't happen all at once. You've got to give it time. Remember, you're new to them. Give them awhile, and I bet it will work out." Andrea shifted her books. "See you after school?"

"Sure," Holly said absentmindedly. "No, wait! I forgot, with all that happened at lunch—I'm meeting Tim after school."

"Ah, Tim! I smell romance in the air." Andrea sighed.

"That's autumn you smell," Holly said and laughed, her bad mood completely gone. Then she added, "Hey—thanks for all your wisdom."

"I'll send you my bill in the morning," quipped Andrea.

During her next class, Holly tried to remember what she had eaten for lunch and couldn't. During world history she wrote the word *Haycroft* on the top of a sheet of paper and then drew two columns, which she headed "Plus" and "Minus." On the "Plus" side she wrote: Beautiful setting, Closer to home, Andrea here. On the "Minus" side she wrote: No one likes me—YET.

Well, she reasoned, at least the pluses outweigh the minuses. She tucked the sheet back into her binder, but not before she had written *Tim* several times in her best calligraphy. The thought of him was the one bright spot in her dismal day.

"How'd it go?" Tim asked as he walked up behind Holly, taking her by surprise. She'd been scanning the grounds for him, and she jumped at the sound of his voice.

"You startled me! I didn't see you when I first came out. It must be the shock of hitting sunshine after a day in those 'hallowed halls.' " The enthusiasm in her voice was partly because of seeing Tim and partly the relief she felt that the school day was finally over.

"That bad, huh?" asked Tim.

"No, not really. I kind of like the buildings. They're so stately—historic. I guess I feel like I should be in a long lace gown when I come down that spiral staircase into the main hall."

"Well, I'm glad you decided against the lace gown. We'd make a pretty strange-looking couple when we stop for a soda." Tim smiled and looked at Holly. The warmth of his gaze made her feel good all over. The sun was shining on his hair, bringing out reddish highlights she hadn't noticed before. For the first time, too, she realized just how dark his brown eyes were.

Now they had reached the busy street. "Do you like to run?" Tim asked.

"Run? Only when I'm in a hurry or when I have to catch a taxi." Tim caught hold of her arm and propelled her at breakneck speed through a break in traffic to the park on the other side of the street.

"Do you always run that fast?" she asked, catching her breath. Tim didn't let go of her arm, and she was glad. His hand was warm and comfortable where it rested.

"I should warn you, I'm on the track team—do wind sprints when I can to keep in shape. So where do you want to go? What would you like to do?" he asked.

Holly grinned at him. "I thought you were planning a night at the opera."

Tim shook his head and laughed. "I have a feeling you're not going to let me forget that. I think I'm beginning to know how your mind works."

They didn't cut straight across the park to town. Instead, they took a roundabout route and found themselves asking questions about each other from family life to food preferences. Tim said he was an only child, like Holly, but his definition meant that his three older brothers were away at college. Holly found that talking to him was easy, natural.

"What are you thinking about?" he asked her after a brief silence.

"I was thinking that if there really was a Hartley Square, it would be just like this." Tim smiled at her, letting her know he understood. Together they walked along the cobblestone path, past a fountain and beside a pond, talking nonstop. Holly's heart was singing. He likes me, she kept repeating to herself. He really does. At that moment nothing else seemed to matter.

Chapter Four

"I don't want to kiss you, but don't take it personally," Holly stammered.

"How else am I supposed to take it?" Billy Gabriel couldn't help laughing. He was also confused. "I've kissed you on your birthday, Christmas, and on New Year's Eve."

"On the cheek! That's not what this scene calls for, and you know it. It makes me feel— uncomfortable, I guess. I'm going to talk to Chris about it."

Holly had five minutes before the seven o'clock dry rehearsal, and she found Chris on the empty set.

"You're a little early, aren't you?" Chris looked up from the script and smiled. If he felt the pressures of being one of three directors on the country's major soap, he rarely showed it.

"Chris, I need to talk to you about scene three B."

He flipped open the script to the exact page, almost without looking. "What's the problem? Looks like a good one for you."

"Well, the kiss part. You know I've never had to do that on-camera before." She didn't dare tell him she had never been kissed off-camera either!

"You know I don't write 'em. I just direct," was his standard line for any script complaints. "Come on, Holly, you're an actress, and a good one. You can do it. Relax. Remember it's only a job. Pretend."

"Pretend what?" she asked.

"That you're kissing your boyfriend," he suggested.

Holly's face colored. Whether Tim was her boyfriend or not, just that reference made her blush.

"*Now* you've got it! The blush is perfect," Chris teased. "See you in exactly three minutes."

She dashed back to the dressing room, gulped from an open bottle of orange juice, and had about two minutes left to consider what Chris had said.

HARTLEY SQUARE
ACT IV, SCENE 3B

[Backstage at the Loose End Disco, outside Jed's dressing room. Group of TEENAGERS excited, talking about performance. LINDSEY looks uncomfortable, casts an annoyed glance at her cousin Sheila.]

SHEILA: What are you so down about? I thought you'd be thrilled when my mother got us these backstage passes. After all, not everyone gets to meet Jed Shine after a show.

LINDSEY: I feel stupid, standing here like some groupie.

SHEILA: *[Spotting Jed in the distance with the other kids, swoons.]* Here he comes! Here, take this extra program. If I can't get his autograph, then you'll have to. *[Afterthought.]* But remember, it's mine if you do!

LINDSEY: *[Interrupting, bored.]* Sure, I know— your mother got the passes. *[Voice trails off among the shouting teens as JED nears.]*

JED: Whoa! Take it easy! Don't break my body. Here you go. *[Signing as many autographs as he can. Makes eye contact with*

Lindsey and smiles. Continues to study her while writing.]

AGENT: That's it, kids. Give Jed a break. He needs some rest. [*Starts ushering kids down the hall. KIDS reluctant. SHEILA preceding, LINDSEY is last.*]

JED: [*Touching Lindsey's arm.*] Hey, you're the only one who didn't ask for my autograph. Was I off-key?

LINDSEY: Oh, no. I loved the performance. I just find scenes like this a little ridiculous.

JED: [*Taking her program and signing it.*] Here—maybe you can give it to a friend.

LINDSEY: Now I'm embarrassed. [*Turns away.*]

JED: Don't be. It's refreshing to meet someone who doesn't follow the crowd. [*Turns her toward him. Impulsively takes her chin and kisses her on the lips. LINDSEY enjoys kiss for the moment but backs off, stunned.*]

JED: What's your name?

LINDSEY: [*Barely able to speak.*] Lindsey.

JED: Beautiful. You and the name. I'll be seeing you, Lindsey.

[*Take. LINDSEY dumbfounded.*]

[*Pan Corridor.* SHEILA *furious.*]

[*Fade out. cut to #3C, Aunt Lydia's town-house, parlor.*]

"That's going to be perfect," Chris said. "Do the same on final taping. No surprises. Only change I want is less swooning from teenagers and more screaming. Remember this is a rock star you're seeing, in person. Show some excitement. Generate!"

Holly felt numb. She had actually done the scene. She wished she could look as casual as Billy, who was tuning his guitar for the final take.

"You did just fine, Holly. I told you not to worry. Tell me," Chris asked quietly, "how did you get yourself psyched for that kiss?"

"Like you said, Chris, I reminded myself that it's only a job." She sounded like a pro. But when she turned to head for makeup, she let herself admit the truth. She had closed her eyes and pretended that Billy was Tim.

Holly's first English-composition assignment at Haycroft had been to describe in a step-by-step format any nonschool project completed in the past year. Holly had chosen to write about what she knew best—taping a segment for a TV soap.

Mrs. Nearing, her English teacher, had decided to read Holly's essay to the class.

Holly felt slightly conspicuous at hearing her own words filling the room. She didn't have to look around the room to know that at least twenty pairs of eyes were fixed on her.

Mrs. Nearing finished reading the composition and said, "Holly, that was an excellent report."

Holly smiled and shifted her position, hoping to feel more comfortable. She only half listened to what Mrs. Nearing was saying. "Excuse me?"

"I asked how long it took you to compose this," Mrs. Nearing repeated.

"Oh, it couldn't have been more than thirty minutes. I wrote it on the train." She was speaking without really thinking. "It was after the industrial area and before the state line, so I guess . . ."

Suddenly everyone was laughing, and she wished the teacher would say something reassuring like, "We're not laughing *at* you but *with* you." She didn't. For the rest of the period, Holly had all she could do to concentrate. One thought kept running through her mind: If I could only write a script for my own life and have things go *my* way for once, like Lindsey. As the bell sounded, she gathered up her books and decided she'd give script writing her best shot. Tune in to "Holly's World," she said to herself.

At her locker she picked up on the general conversation between Amanda and the girls whose names all sounded alike.

"Written after the industrial zone. Imagine what she could do with the marshland as inspiration!" More giggling.

"An A plus and I work two hours and get a rotten C! I wonder if teachers always give stars to stars."

"Next time," Amanda said to one of her friends, "you've got to come up with a project more exciting than making an afghan. Maybe you should launch a career in TV, for example." She said TV with scornful emphasis.

Holly spun around. "You make afghans? Hailey, isn't it?" Hailey nodded. "Now that's a talent I'd like to have. Maybe you could show me how sometime," Holly suggested brightly.

She closed her locker and started past the girls. "Oh, Amanda," she gushed, "I *really* like that blouse. I can never wear beige. It washes me out. You're lucky."

She didn't turn to look, but she could almost hear the jaws dropping. She sailed

43

through the rest of the day, determined to win over the most popular girls. Andrea was puzzled by Holly's sudden turnaround.

"What's up, Holly? Why all this sweetness to everyone? You're acting pretty weird all of a sudden."

"It's the new me." Holly laughed. "See you Monday!"

Not a bad day, Holly mused. She walked home alone since Andrea's father was picking her up after school to spend the weekend with him in New York City. Holly was pleased with her performance that day at Haycroft. But now and Saturday night she could be herself. She was going out with Tim on Saturday, and he had said the entire evening would be a surprise. She closed her eyes for an instant and wondered what it would be like to be actually kissed by Tim. . . .

Chapter Five

They had driven almost twenty miles, and Holly was more than surprised when Tim stopped his car in front of a small restaurant called The Opera.

"Told you I'd keep my promise," he said, laughing at Holly's expression. "A night at The Opera, OK?"

"You're—you're something else!" Holly burst out laughing.

"You, too," he said, giving her a warm smile. "Well, we'd better go in and see what this night at The Opera has in store."

They sat at a small table for two in a corner. Holly thought the red-checkered table-cloths were right out of a studio set, and when they looked up and saw a smiling waiter with a large mustache beaming down at them, they could barely keep straight faces.

When he left they broke up. "He's *got* to be an actor," Holly said. "He's absolutely typecast as the Italian waiter."

They shared a thick, crusty pizza, which the restaurant called "rustica." It was topped with everything from anchovies to black olives. Holly savored every bite. Nothing had ever tasted so good.

Tim reached for his third slice. "Tell me about your job. Do you like it?" he asked.

Holly nearly choked and reached for her water. "I'm sorry," she said when she recovered. "It's just that no one has ever asked me that before or said it quite that way."

"I don't understand." He looked confused.

"No one calls it a job. That's the way *I* think of it. But most people think it's all glamour, not work. And what they usually ask are personal questions about cast members—the gossip."

"I get it." Tim winked. "So how do you like your job?"

"I like it a lot," she replied, and they both grinned.

"Do you ever get bored doing the same thing every day? I know *I* do. There are days when I never want to see another grapefruit, let alone stack them in a pyramid."

"No, that's just it. You're not doing the same play every day, saying the same lines. Every day is different." Holly was so obviously delighted to talk about her work that Tim sat quietly and let her finish.

"You know, sometimes the story can be repetitious. There are times when you have to repeat what went on the week before, just in case someone missed a program or two. But mostly, it's all new—like an unfolding of what happens in each person's life. Some people criticize, saying the plots are dumb, but I think it's a way of leaving reality for a while. And that can be healthy—" She stopped and looked up. "I'm talking too much."

"No, it's OK. You've just given me a whole new outlook on soap operas. I've been stealing looks at you on the TV in the back room at work," Tim said and studied a radiant Holly. "You certainly don't look like you need an escape from reality. I'd say your life seems pretty perfect."

"At this very moment it is." Holly smiled at him. She didn't want to spoil the mood by telling him about the things that weren't so perfect in her life, namely her new school and lack of friends.

Holly quickly changed the subject to Tim. He told her all about Amsbly, modestly describing his achievements on the track team and telling funny stories about his friends. He suddenly had her wishing she could be part of his world.

"You know," he said thoughtfully, "I wish I could spring for dinners like this all the time. It's so much fun. But Mr. White is a firm believer in the minimum wage."

"Don't apologize. It's more important to me to be having a good time and being with someone I like than going out to a lot of fancy places." Holly amazed herself, sounding so wise.

"You know what we just said without exactly saying it?" Tim asked.

"What?"

"That we want to see more of each other no matter what we do or where we go."

"I guess we did." She flushed. Tim broke an awkward silence by calling for the check.

When he took her home and walked her to the front door, they were laughing again; this time about Tim's dog showing up at a track meet, following Tim, and then beating him to the finish line.

"That's a Charlie Brown story if I ever heard one. Don't tell me your dog's name is Snoopy, or I'll know you're making it up," Holly warned him, smiling.

Instead of answering, he bent down and kissed her—lightly, as though he were afraid she'd misinterpret his sudden move. "You have the most fantastic brown eyes," he said softly.

Holly wanted to say something about their wonderful evening and how much she loved his company, but the words wouldn't come. She was silently making a memory of her first *real* kiss. She was dimly aware of Tim saying all the right words about their evening together and promising to call the next day. Wrapped in a rosy cloud, Holly just nodded.

"Hey," he called as he headed down the walkway. Holly was almost inside the door. "Road Runner—my dog's name!"

"For real?" she asked, like a child afraid of being teased.

"For real." He laughed and watched her go inside.

Holly closed the front door and leaned against it, reliving the moment when his lips had touched hers. For the moment, at least, everything was perfect in "Holly's World."

In her sleep that night Holly watched the faces of people in her life changing as the glass chips in a kaleidoscope do. First there was Amanda, then images of some other girls at school, Andrea, and finally, Tim. They began flashing faster and faster before her, and the distant murmurings she heard grew louder until they became screeching laughter. Holly bolted upright, wide awake and shivering. Clutching the comforter around her, she settled back down.

To blot out the nightmare, she tried recalling her date with Tim. But even that warm memory could not stop her shivering. The face of Tim laughing at her kept popping into her mind. Would he, she wondered, stop liking her if he knew she was not popular at school—that she had only one real friend?

Now she was more determined than ever to win over the girls at Haycroft in order to impress Tim with the fact that she was just like any other girl. She remembered how "Holly's World" had worked the other day at school. If she planned it right, it could keep working. At last she dozed off and woke up a few hours later feeling refreshed. Holly checked the clock. Good, it wasn't too early to call Andrea at her father's apartment. She grabbed the phone and dialed, ready to put her plan into action.

"Hi! It's Holly. Are you awake?"

"Barely. But I grabbed the phone so it wouldn't disturb my father. Dad's weekends are going to total me! He finds more elaborate things to do each time. I told him I'd be just as happy sitting around here with him, having dinner and watching a movie on TV or something." Andrea sounded sleepy.

"Where'd you go?" Holly asked, but there was no answer. "Andrea, *wake up!*"

"Sorry," she said, yawning. "Where *did* we go? Oh, yeah. First we went to the top of the World Trade Center for dinner. My ears are still popping. Then we went for a carriage ride in the park. The horse smelled. Then we went to some famous ice cream parlor on Central Park South, but I can't remember the name. And *then* we caught a late movie on Fifty-seventh Street."

"Sounds exhausting! How can he ever top a weekend like that? Maybe it was the finale, and next time you'll just send out for pizza and sit in front of the TV," Holly said, trying to reassure her friend.

"Not likely. Why are you calling me here, anyway? It's long distance, you know."

"I want you to do me a favor."

"If it's a plastic replica of the World Trade Center, you've already got it. I bought you one yesterday. Dad insisted I take back a souvenir for one of my 'little friends.'" Andrea groaned.

Ordinarily Holly would have broken up over Andrea's remark, but she was too involved with her own plans. "Tomorrow after school I have make-up work to do for biology. I want you to sign me up for the Halloween dance committee and wait for me till I get to the meeting."

"What? Why on earth would you want to be on that committee? It's mostly Amanda and her friends who will plan the dance. I thought you didn't like that crowd."

"Please, Andrea, just do it for me. It's important," Holly persisted.

"Am I imagining all this?" Andrea asked.

"No. And, please, just say you'll do it."

"OK. Now I think I want to go back to sleep," Andrea mumbled. "Dad said something about doing two museums and the zoo today." She hung up the phone, and Holly heard the hum of the dial tone.

She replaced the receiver and curled up under the pink comforter. When she closed her eyes, she was able to bring back the memory of Tim's kiss. I have a boyfriend, she thought dreamily, and a best friend, and soon I'll make the girls at Haycroft like me, too.

Chapter Six

Someone had just suggested burning the teachers in effigy in a roaring bonfire. Everyone was laughing as Holly entered the room. There was some buzzing when she came in, but Holly let it pass and flashed her best on-camera smile. The Halloween dance committee meeting was nearly over, with only decorations and food left to be discussed.

There was an empty seat next to Andrea, but Holly deliberately chose a different one. I'm not going to lean on Andrea, she said to herself. I've got to do this on my own.

Amanda was speaking. "Come on, let's be serious. No more burning teachers. Think of some way to make the dining hall look spooky."

Holly plunged in. "What about converting the dining hall—inside and out—into a haunted mansion?" Even Andrea's eyebrows were raised. There were immediate questions as to how they would go about such a massive undertaking.

Everyone was looking at her with interest. It was the first time Holly had ever had their attention, and she was going to play the scene for all it was worth.

"Our network has a warehouse of props in the city," she began. "I know I could borrow enough to make the dining hall really spooky. They have these mechanical monsters that are so lifelike. We could put one of them at the entrance. And then there are bats on fine wires, activated by a wind machine. Maybe I could borrow a special light to create eerie shadows."

Amanda was quickly scribbling notes, nodding at every item Holly mentioned. "How soon do you think you could get all that, Holly?" She was not using the sarcastic tone she usually reserved for Holly but a more pleasant one.

"The longest I could have them for would be twenty-four hours, so I'd have to pick up everything the morning of the dance and return them the next morning. It'll be OK, though—my dad would be able to pick up everything in one of his company vans." Not that she'd asked him, but she was sure he'd do it. As for the props, that wouldn't be a problem. She knew they hadn't been used for years. Holly hadn't felt so pleased with herself in ages.

After the meeting Hailey, who was in charge of refreshments, asked Holly for suggestions. Holly was still on her creative streak and came up with the idea of a witch's brew of hot cider in a caldron. Hailey was delighted and thanked Holly—even asking if she could call her for the recipe. The only one who wasn't wildly enthusiastic was Andrea.

On the walk home Holly was still excited, talking about the dance. "Maybe we should put another monster outside the dining hall," she said, musing out loud.

Andrea stopped, looked at her friend, and shook her head. "Holly, don't you think that maybe you went just a little too far in there, making all those promises? For a moment I thought you were doing a Lindsey dialogue."

"Stop looking so grim. Of course I can get the props. It's as good as in the can."

Andrea looked puzzled and then remembered. "Oh, show biz talk. It's either a 'wrap' or 'in the can.' Do you think you could rejoin reality for a minute and tell me what's going to happen if those monsters don't materialize?"

"What's got you so down today?" Holly asked, annoyed that her friend didn't share her enthusiasm.

"Nothing. I'm just afraid you'll fall on your face, and I'm wondering why you're trying so hard to impress girls you couldn't stand last week. You know, Amanda and her group aren't the only kids in this school. There are a lot of others you could get to know."

"Maybe I did get a little carried away," Holly admitted, "but you have to understand something. I'm tired of always being on the fringes of school life. I want to find out what it's like on the *inside*."

"I guess I understand. It's just that you seem to want everything to happen immediately—yesterday, for that matter," said Andrea.

"I'm tired of waiting. I want things to start happening *now*!"

"I just hope it works out, Holly," Andrea said quietly.

"Thanks. Are you OK? You really do look beat."

"It's my parents again, I guess. My mother's mad because Dad brought me back home late last night, and they had a big shouting match. I hate it when that happens." Andrea cradled her books in her arms, her chin resting on the edge of her binder.

"I'm sorry. I forget all you're going through." Holly wished she could say something to make her friend feel better, but she was at a loss for words.

"It's OK. It's just that sometimes I feel like the candy in a taffy pull, going in two directions at once." Andrea's eyes filled, but she blinked back her tears and straightened up.

They had reached the corner where they would part. "I'll call you tonight, and we'll talk about it," Holly said as her friend turned to walk away.

"See ya," Andrea said glumly.

I'll call her right after supper, thought Holly. Suddenly her own problems seemed very small in comparison to Andrea's.

But she never got to call Andrea that night. First Amanda phoned to talk about the dance plans. She even asked Holly's advice on whether an orange dress would clash with her hair. Next Hailey called, and they were on the phone most of the evening. After discussing the recipe for a cider punch, they got silly thinking of names for the rest of the menu—monster burgers, ghosted cheese sandwiches. Holly drew the line at chocolate chip ice cream being called "eye of toad."

By the time Holly hung up the phone, it was time to go to bed if she wanted to look rested for her seven AM rehearsal. She had not only forgotten to call Andrea, but it had completely slipped her mind that Tim had promised to call and the phone had been busy all evening. Drowsily she decided to talk to Andrea during lunch at school. And if Tim had tried to call and hadn't been able to get through, he'd know what a popular person she was, which would make her more interesting to him. Everything would work out fine, Holly was sure of it.

Holly was awake the next morning and nearly dressed before her alarm went off. She wanted to get to the studio early to ask the prop man, Stan, about borrowing the things she needed for the dance. She pulled on jeans and an extra heavy fisherman's knit sweater and slipped into her favorite penny loafers. The house was quiet as she went downstairs. For an instant she panicked, thinking her father might have forgotten that he had said he'd drive her into the city. But there he was at the kitchen table, a mug of coffee in his hands.

"Holly," her father said between sips, "I was just going to wake you. Why are you dressed so early? We have more than half an hour before we have to leave."

"No, we don't. Daddy, please get dressed. Remember, I told you I wanted to be a little early to talk to Stan?"

"Stan? Oh, yeah," he said, still somewhat groggy. "I still don't like you committing me to requisitioning one of the vans to drive monsters to your school dance, especially monsters you don't have yet. Aren't you putting the cart before the horse?"

"But you'll do it? Please, Daddy. It's important."

He sighed. "All right. And you can stop blinking those big saucer eyes at me. You've charmed me again."

When he left to dress, Holly packed a banana and a peanut butter granola bar into her makeup bag. She'd eat in the car.

With no traffic on the road, she was at the studio by six-thirty. Five minutes later she'd located Stan and made her request. His response devastated her.

"No way, kid. Sorry, but no can do," he told her.

"But, Stan, I'll look like a fool in front of

59

the entire school! I *promised* I'd get the props."
Holly was near tears.

"Honey, I'd help you out if I could. But why did you promise anything without asking me? The monsters—all the stuff you mentioned—are being used on that kids' program Halloween Day. The 'Jolly Jack Show' —that's the one. And it's taped the same day, so there's no way you can have them."

Holly was crushed, and Stan's sympathy didn't help. "Hey," he called after her as she headed disconsolately for the dressing room wing, "I'll throw a sheet over myself and come as a ghost if that will help." His booming laugh echoed in the half-empty cavernous studio, but Holly didn't feel in the least like laughing.

In the dressing room wing a mellow sound filled the empty hallway. Billy had come in early, Holly guessed, to practice the song he would sing that day as Jed Shine's new hit. His voice was strong but gentle and soothing, too.

> *How do I reach you*
> *When you won't listen to me?*
> *How can I hold you*
> *When you want to be free?*
> *You tell me you love me*

But then kiss me goodbye.
You tell me you don't care,
But then you still cry.

He picked up the tempo when he reached the refrain.

What can I do,
What can I say
To try and get you, girl,
To see it my way?

Listening to him sing, Holly had a brainstorm. She burst into his dressing room before he could repeat the refrain. She had an idea that could save the Haycroft dance and make her a heroine rather than a fool.

"Billy, please, could you do me a big favor?" she asked breathlessly.

"Holly, I came in early especially to practice—when it's all quiet with no one bouncing into my dressing room begging for favors." But he really wasn't angry, and Holly knew it.

She told him what had happened with the props she'd so rashly promised to provide, and she also told him something about her situation at Haycroft.

"You ought to be the most popular girl in school," he said sincerely. "But I didn't get into this business until I was out of school, so I guess I can understand that some kids would resent your living a life that must seem like a dreamworld to them. Sometimes I think about how lucky I am being a part of all this. Keeps me humble."

Holly laughed with him, then returned to the topic that was foremost in her mind. "The favor I started to ask you for—"

He interrupted. "Don't ask me to speak to Stan, Holly. I barely know the guy. If the props aren't available, that's it. There's nothing I can do." He struck a chord on his guitar like a musical exclamation point.

"That's not what I wanted to ask you. What I want—" she hesitated, "is to know if you'd consider coming to the dance and singing for us." Before he could open his mouth, Holly hurried on. "All the girls are crazy about Jed Shine—about *you*, I mean. It would be the biggest thing to happen at Haycroft since —I don't know—since the former headmistress ran off with the gardener!"

Billy was laughing. "OK, Holly-baby. Here's what we'll do. I'll try to get there, but if something comes up, like if my agent gets me an engagement for that weekend, I won't be able to make it."

Holly leaped up and gave him a hug.

"Remember I said *try*, so don't go promising anybody I'm coming and put yourself deeper in a hole if I don't make it."

"I promise," she said, "and I'll never forget your wanting to do this for me! And I *loved* your song!" She gave him another quick hug, which evidently embarrassed him.

"Now will you get out of here and let me practice?" He frowned, then smiled at her as she left the room.

She walked into her own dressing room, leaving the door ajar. Billy began singing again:

> *What can I do,*
> *What can I say*
> *To try and get you, girl,*
> *To see it my way?*

Yes, Holly said to herself, no dumb mechanical monster can top that voice. The girls will absolutely *die*! If only I could tell them— but no. Billy's right. I've just got to keep my big mouth shut for once, and cross my fingers.

Chapter Seven

Fall seemed to have arrived overnight in a breathtaking blaze of color. Holly had been so busy the past few weeks, she had hardly noticed the landscape. Looking out her bedroom window, she allowed herself a few minutes to appreciate the beauty of the season. Down in the yard, her father was raking fallen leaves onto an old sheet. Ordinarily she would be helping him, but she needed some time to herself.

The window seat was her favorite thinking place. As a child she could stretch out on it. Now she rested her chin on her knees and wrapped her arms around them. She was thinking of the Halloween dance that night and was so filled with anticipation she thought she'd burst. If only he showed up! Having

Billy there would make up—*more* than make up—for the decorations disaster and the awful scene she'd faced when she had told the committee there would be no props coming from the studio.

Holly had watched Amanda's face go rigid when she told the committee she had failed.

"I knew it! You probably made the whole thing up to impress us," Amanda said, fuming, and banged the table with her fist in a decisive gesture. "I vote Holly off the committee!"

There were some murmurings of agreement, but Holly observed that they were not unanimous.

"Give her a break, Amanda." It was Carley who spoke. "Let's at least hear what she has to say."

Holly felt she had won a round. Instead of being flushed and flustered, she slipped into her Lindsey characterization and turned on a woeful look. Her heartfelt apology drew the sympathy she'd hoped for, although Amanda still looked skeptical.

"Why don't we make the best of this and come up with our own decorations? I'll work hard to help," Holly said pleadingly.

Somehow it worked, and Holly kept her place on the committee. Just thinking about it now gave her a chill. How many times she had wanted to blurt out the secret that Billy was coming! But she didn't. It was probably the hardest secret she'd ever kept. Only her parents knew about it, but her exhilaration about the dance was heavily laced with guilt because she hadn't told Tim.

What was worse, she'd had to refuse Tim's offer to go with him to a dance at Amsbly. She remembered vividly the day he'd asked her. Tim had had track practice, and she had gone over to Amsbly High to watch him. Hurrying to get there on time, she ran part of the way and was red-faced and panting when he met her.

"Hey, I'm the one on the track team, remember? I thought you only ran for taxi cabs." He laughed and hugged her.

"Maybe you're converting me," she said, joking. "Yesterday I felt like running down an empty corridor at school and nearly knocked a teacher down when I rounded a corner."

"You watch out you don't get a ticket for reckless running! Listen, sit over there. I have something I want to ask you after." He waved back twice as he ran to the field.

Holly watched him, smooth and graceful in each stride. Later he did a hundred-yard dash that won him slaps on the back from his teammates. But still later when he came out of the locker room wearing jeans, a heavy sweater, and a wide grin, he looked anything but tired.

"I don't know how you do it," Holly said admiringly.

"Sheer stamina—good food, clean living—"

"Oh, stop teasing! You were sensational, and I want to see you in a meet sometime."

"You will, I promise. But promise me something else first—that you'll come to the Amsbly Halloween dance with me."

Holly's heart leaped for joy, then sank like a stone. She would have given anything to be able to be Tim's date, but she'd promised to help serve refreshments at the Haycroft dance, and besides, she had to be there to welcome Billy—if he appeared. For an instant she thought of asking Tim to go to her dance, then decided against it. If everything worked out and Billy actually performed, she'd be obligated to spend all her time with him, making introductions and fending off adoring fans. It wouldn't be much fun for Tim, and anyway, he might not believe that her relationship with Billy was purely business. She just couldn't risk it. So she muttered something about her responsibility to the dance committee, and Tim, though obviously disappointed, told her he understood. He was so sweet about it that Holly wanted to cry. It was all she could do to keep from blurting out her secret, but the timing would have been all wrong. How could she explain why it was so important to be accepted and admired by the other girls at Haycroft?

After the dance is over, she said to herself, I'll tell him everything, and he'll understand. Holly glanced at the dress hanging on her closet door. It was a deep rust velvet that she had worn once on the show. She'd borrowed it from wardrobe and would have to bring it back on Monday. It was absolutely perfect—if only Tim could see her in it! What if he went to the Amsbly dance alone and met somebody else? What if Billy didn't show? What if . . .

Holly leaped to her feet. All those "what ifs" were driving her crazy. She grabbed her jacket and ran downstairs. Better to rake leaves than to sit there tying herself in knots!

By seven-thirty on Halloween night, Holly was dressed in the rust velvet and was nervously pacing the living room. There had been no word at all from Billy, and Holly was due at Haycroft at eight o'clock. Her parents, never having seen her so keyed up, found it hard to understand why she was so determined to impress her new friends.

"You look lovely, dear," said Mrs. Giles as

Holly ran to the window for the twentieth time, looking for some sign of Billy. "Exactly like Lindsey. You've been acting very Lindsey-ish lately, too, I've noticed."

"Frankly, I prefer Holly Giles," her father added. "She's just as pretty, but she's not nearly so hyper."

"How does Tim feel about this business with Billy?" asked Mrs. Giles. "Doesn't he think it's kind of strange that you're going to the dance with somebody else?"

"Oh, Mom, *please!*" said Holly. "You just don't understand. I haven't told him. I have my reasons."

Her parents exchanged worried glances, but just then there was a ring of the doorbell, and Holly jumped as though she'd been shot. "Oh, I hope it's Billy! I hope, I hope . . ." she muttered as she ran to open the door.

It was. He'd arrived in a rented limousine, which looked about a block long, and told Holly and her parents that he needed it in order to get back to Manhattan by eleven-thirty because he was appearing at a small rock club. After a brief conversation with Mr. and Mrs. Giles, Billy helped Holly into her coat, and they stepped out into the crisp October night. Holly was so excited she could hardly speak. This would do it, she was certain. She'd never be an outsider at Haycroft again!

Holly and Billy's arrival at the dance equaled the flurry of a Hollywood premiere. The school photographer began snapping away as soon as they entered the building, and they were immediately surrounded by the Haycroft girls and their dates. Amanda took Holly aside to ask in a whisper if she and Billy were going together, to which Holly replied, with a Lindsey smile, that they were just good friends.

When Billy was finally able to get away from the admiring crowd in order to perform, every number was punctuated with sighs and squeals of delight. His final number was the new song Holly had heard him rehearsing at the studio. He dedicated it to the Haycroft girls, and when the song was over, the dining hall vibrated with applause.

"Aren't you the sneaky one!" said Carley, poking Holly in the ribs. "You had this planned all along!"

Holly smiled—mysteriously, she hoped. "Maybe," was all she said.

The only upsetting thing about the entire evening was that Andrea seemed to be deliberately avoiding Holly, obviously hurt that she hadn't been let in on the secret. I'll make it up to her, Holly promised herself. Tomorrow, or the next day. But I'm not going to let her spoil tonight.

Even after Billy left, after signing dozens of autographs, the magic continued. Everyone flocked around Holly, congratulating her on making the dance the biggest success ever. If only Tim could be here, she thought with a pang, but then another group surrounded her, and she was caught up in the excitement of the moment.

Monday, the talk at Haycroft was still of the dance. In the afternoon someone found a copy of the local newspaper with Holly and Billy's picture on the front page and a headline over the article, "NIGHT OF STARS AT HAYCROFT." After world history class, Amanda caught up with Holly midway down the spiral staircase.

"We all want to go downtown after school and get some copies of the newspaper. Can you believe that, thanks to you, the newspaper printed the names of the *committee members* for the dance?"

"I didn't have anything to do with that," Holly said honestly.

"Your picture with Billy did it! I wouldn't be surprised if one of the city papers picked

it up. Listen, come to town with us later."
Amanda didn't wait for an answer. She seemed
to float down the stairs, her red hair flaring
behind her.

Holly smiled to herself, feeling quite pleased
with all she'd accomplished in such a short
time at Haycroft. She continued on downstairs and spotted Andrea walking toward the
gym.

"Andrea, wait up!" Andrea stopped but
didn't turn around.

"Hey," Holly said, "where did you get to
at lunchtime? I couldn't find you. And what
was the disappearing act you pulled at the
dance Saturday all about? I looked all over
for you, but you were gone."

Andrea turned, and Holly saw the anger
in her face. "I felt like eating outdoors today
to get away from all the dance talk. You've
certainly become the center of attraction at
Haycroft."

"What's wrong with that? If you're my
true friend, I'd think you'd be happy I'm starting to make new friends."

"It's the way you're going about it!" Andrea's face was fiery now. "You're not yourself
anymore. I don't know *who* you are, but at
the dance you were really showing off."

"Maybe you're just jealous. Maybe you

don't want me to have other friends." Holly was angry now, too.

"Jealous? I'm trying to keep you from acting like a jerk. Look, I have enough coming down on me right now with my parents. I don't think I can handle the new you. Maybe you should get yourself another best friend— get a hundred if you want—*Lindsey!*" She turned and stormed off.

Holly felt two emotions at once—hurt and anger. She comforted herself with the fact that she and Andrea had had arguments before but always smoothed them over. Still, Andrea had never accused her of showing off before!

Just as Holly was trying to figure whether Andrea's calling her Lindsey had any significance, she was distracted by someone calling her name.

"Come on, let's get to town before the newspapers are sold out!" It was Carley, who was with Amanda and Hailey.

"Sure, I'm ready," Holly said and joined them. She surprised herself at finally being able to keep the girls' names straight.

In town the girls headed for Drapkin's, the news and stationery store. Coming down the street in the opposite direction was Tim. Holly called out to him and ran ahead of the others, hoping to catch him before he entered White's Grocery Store.

"Hi," she said cheerfully. "I'm so glad I got to see you before you went to work. I wanted to talk to you about the other night—"

"It's OK," he said stiffly. He wasn't smiling.

"You understand then. I knew you would," she said, sighing with relief.

"I don't know what there is to understand, but the next time you have a date with another guy, you could at least say so." Tim slammed the newspaper he was holding into his other hand. "Look, I don't like being manipulated like some character on 'Hartley Square'!"

"It wasn't a date. I was—" Holly was interrupted by the girls calling her to hurry up.

"I've got to run—my friends are waiting." Holly was torn between wanting to talk to Tim and not wanting the girls to walk in on an awkward conversation.

"Sure. Your friends," he said sarcastically, then stormed into the grocery store, leaving Holly staring miserably after him.

"Don't tell me," Amanda said when Holly had slowly rejoined the group. "He wanted your autograph."

"No, nothing like that," Holly said, looking back at the store.

"Well, all this local publicity can't hurt your social life. And you can bet the boys from Lloyd Prep who were at the dance have seen the newspaper."

"Look, I'm not interested. I don't even know anything about Lloyd Prep. Let's just go get the papers."

"Hailey's getting us a bunch right now," Amanda said and winked at one of the other girls.

"Then I'd better go and give her some money for mine," Holly said, reaching into her bag.

"Never mind." Amanda laughed. "It's on the house." With that, she and Carley nudged each other, sharing some private joke. Holly didn't understand but attempted a giddy giggle anyway.

No one was at home when Holly arrived there after school. Her mother was at some sort of seminar for women planning to reenter the job market, and her father was still at work in the city. Holly used the time alone to try and put together the pieces of her day. Nothing fit.

She walked into the family room and turned on a low light. Then she flopped down on the maroon leather sofa and crossed her legs in a semi-yoga position. She looked at the opposite wall—the trophy wall, her father called it. It held photographs of Holly, stills made on the set of HS showing the soft smile and wide eyes that revealed a glimmer of the woman who would some day emerge. Photographs of Holly or of Lindsey? Holly suddenly wondered. In one day, Holly thought, I've lost my best friend, had my first argument with Tim, and become a star at school! She looked up at the teenage Lindsey again and swore she bore no resemblance to that spoiled, emotional girl.

"It was just a bad day," she said out loud. But inside, she realized that the script of "Holly's World" she had created for herself had some holes in it. I'll fix it all up tomorrow, she said to herself, and leaned her head back. Everything always looks better in the morning. . . .

Chapter Eight

"Your face is beginning to look like a map of the Yangtze River with all its tributaries."

The photographer was right. The makeup man had put too much foundation on Holly, and under the hot lights it was streaking. Ordinarily she would have left the set after her scene for HS was finished. But that day she had to remain for a magazine interview and photographs.

As Amanda had predicted, a city news-paper had picked up the item about Holly and Billy at the school dance. *Bottom Line* magazine, in turn, had picked up on the news report and arranged an interview through the soap's press representative.

Holly had given interviews before, usually about her home life and her role on the show. But that day's interview had a different focus—Holly and Billy, and whether or not they were a duo both on and off screen. She was having trouble fielding questions and for the first time in an interview looked to the show's press representative, Shawn Mullen, for help. The reporter seemed to enjoy watching Holly fumble.

"Holly, you just said that you and Billy are only friends, and yet he traveled all the way to a school dance in the suburbs and was pictured with his arm around you?"

"Well, yes," Holly said tonelessly.

"Yes, what—friends or more than friends?" The reporter, a woman in her mid-thirties, was very much in control. Holly felt like a small child by comparison.

Shawn interceded. "What Holly means is that she and Billy have been friends for more than a year since he joined HS. You have to understand that the whole cast is like a big family."

"A family? Does that make Holly and Billy like a brother and sister or like a husband and—"

"Oh, come on! Give her a break. She's only fifteen years old! She asked Billy to the dance so her friends at school could hear him sing." Shawn spoke easily and was careful not to alienate the reporter. "The cast does favors for one another all the time."

"Just like in a family," Holly said, regaining her confidence. She finished the rest of the interview without Shawn's help.

"You handled the bloodhound pretty well," he told her later. "Unfortunately, no matter what we say, she'll twist it just enough to suit her needs."

"You mean she'll make Billy and me an 'item' even if it's not true? It's not fair!"

"No, but it sells magazines. You'll probably make the cover." He patted her shoulder and hurried to catch up with one of the "doctors" in the cast.

He's right, Holly realized. *Bottom Line* did sell over a million. It was on every checkout counter in the country—including White's. The girls at Haycroft will be in shock to see me on the cover! Andrea will want to know every detail of the interview. That will help patch things up between us, she thought. But Tim! He's going to be furious. I've got to find some way of convincing him that the interview isn't important, that he's the only one I care about. How can I make him believe me?

She touched her hand to her cheek. Her fingers were covered with the thick, orange-colored foundation. First, she reminded herself, I take the makeup off. Then I think of a way to show Tim he's the guy for me.

Holly's problems at Haycroft seemed to be completely solved. After she told them about the interview, Amanda and the girls were as enthused about it and the cover as Holly had anticipated. She was deluged with invitations to parties, sleep-overs, and shopping trips.

Before gym class, Andrea, standing in her gym uniform, looked more sad than angry. Holly decided it was a good time to try and pave the way back to friendship.

"I wanted to apologize," Holly said meekly.

"For what? I'm the one who said too much." Andrea undid and retied her sneaker as she spoke.

"Well, I guess I did get a little carried away," Holly admitted.

"Oh, Holly. I don't think you really know what I was trying to tell you that day." Andrea shook her head in disbelief and then softened her expression. "Look, let's just forget about it for now. It's no time for me to go poking into someone else's head when my own isn't on straight."

"That's fine with me. I don't think I could

stand having you mad at me for very long. I need you, Andrea, I really do."

The rest of the gym class was beginning to trickle in from the locker room. The teacher, Mrs. Rymer, appeared with her clipboard and blew a sharp blast on her whistle. Andrea and Holly joined the line of girls in dark green shorts and crisp white shirts with Haycroft over the heart.

Holly whispered to Andrea, "I've got a lot to tell you. I had an interview with *Bottom Line* yesterday, and they're using me on the cover!" She watched Andrea's face brighten. "I'll tell you about it tonight after I patch things up with Tim."

Andrea moved closer to Holly without taking her eyes off Mrs. Rymer. "Patch things up? Why? What's wrong?"

"I'll explain everything tonight."

"As our story unfolds," Andrea said, starting to laugh, "we will find out why Happy Holly is once more extracting her foot from her mouth."

They giggled too loud and caught Mrs. Rymer's icy stare. As she straightened to attention, Holly smiled to herself. It was good to be friends with Andrea again.

*   *   *

Rule number one: Never telephone a boy. Where have I heard that? Holly wondered as she looked in the phone book under the name Hartley. She located the number and then remembered who had made up the rule. It was Aunt Lydia, she thought, laughing to herself. Auntie, as she was known on HS, was the matriarch of the TV family around whom every life in the show revolved.

Well, Aunt Lydia, she thought as the phone was ringing, I'm breaking your rule. "Hi, Tim? Is that you?"

"Holly?"

"Yes." She couldn't think of a way to begin. There was silence at the other end. She had to start somewhere. "I'm calling—uh, you were so angry the other day. I wanted to explain everything to you."

"Yes, I was angry, and if there was an explanation, it should have been made before the dance. Look, you're a free agent. You can go to a dance with anyone you want, but you didn't have to lie to me. How do you think I felt? I thought we could be honest with each other. Trust, it's called."

"Oh, Tim, I *do* trust you, and I want you to trust me. I want to explain why—"

"Do you know what a fool I felt like? All my friends knowing I've been seeing you and then having your picture with that guy in the paper?" Tim was in high gear now, and there was no stopping him. "I didn't mind the ribbing I was getting about a Hartley dating someone from 'Hartley Square'—I can deal with that. But when some of the kids started talking about my competition, it was too much."

"Billy's *not* your competition! I wanted to tell you all about it when I ran into you outside the store the other day, but I didn't want the girls barging into our conversation." Holly went on to tell him why Billy had escorted her to the dance and why it had to be kept a secret. Her voice was trembling. She was afraid she was going to cry.

"I understand why you had to keep it a secret at school. But, Holly, you could have told *me*. I wouldn't have said anything to anyone. It's trust again, Holly."

"I'm sorry, Tim. I really am. Of course I should have told you and Andrea. I feel so stupid!"

"Hey, I've got a suggestion." His voice had softened. "Let's try to put this all behind us. I'm going to be honest with you—as angry as I was, I missed you."

"I've missed seeing you, too." She was cheering up.

"Then let's think of something fun to do together."

Holly thought fast and got an idea. "How would you like to come to 'Hartley Square'?"

"You mean our town park that you've renamed?"

"No, I mean the broadcast studio. See what really goes on, and meet Billy and my other friends there. That way you'll see for yourself that there's nothing between Billy and me."

"It sounds like fun. OK, let's do it. You've seen where I work; it's only right that I see your place of business," he said, laughing.

Holly sighed with relief. She hadn't lost him after all!

Tim would have one day free that week, when Amsbly High was closed for parent-teacher conferences, and he agreed to meet Holly and ride the train with her into the city.

"Six in the morning! How do you do it?" Tim asked when Holly told him what train they would be taking. "Why can't you have an ordinary after-school job like everybody else?"

She laughed. "See you on Thursday."

"Wear something bright so I can spot you on the platform. I don't see too well that early," Tim joked.

Chapter Nine

Tim crept up slowly behind Holly as she stood on the train platform Thursday morning. "You've got good taste, lady," he said softly.

Holly jumped and spun around. He was wearing a bright red woolen pathfinder jacket exactly like hers. They broke into smiles at the same instant, and it was unspoken, but felt, that the day was off to a happy start.

The first thing Tim did when they arrived inside the studio was to entangle himself in the labyrinth of cables on the floor.

"How many broken ankles a day do you people get?" He wrestled himself free of the coiled cable.

"We get used to it," Holly said. "In a long gown or robe it can be tricky."

"Yeah, I can see that. There's a nurse over there."

"She's an extra—an actress for the hospital scenes. Nobody's ever been really hurt on the set that I recall," Holly told him.

She was proud to be showing him around and introducing him to the people she had worked with for three years.

"There's a good feeling here. So—are temperamental stars a myth?" Tim asked after he met the show's Aunt Lydia.

"There's very little time or patience for temperament around here. You'll see later when I'm taping. Everything is happening so fast there's no time for tantrums." And later in the morning, when she left him in the control room to watch her tape, he understood what she meant.

The control room was dark and too tiny for all the equipment it contained. Tim managed to find a space for himself near the door. In front of him was a table that reminded him of the cockpit of a plane. The camera controls were being operated by one man. Others seated near him wore earphones and spoke a language in code that seemed as fast as that of an auctioneer at a county fair. In front of them were a series of TV screens, one for each of the three cameras to be used.

Tim was dazed as he saw three different angles of Aunt Lydia at one time. He was trying to interpret the assistant director's orders, but it was all happening too fast.

"Five—four—three—two—one—cue Aunt Lydia—ready two, shoulder—ready one, pan to Lindsey." And suddenly Tim was seeing Holly perform. What amazed him was he really believed she *was* Lindsey, not just Holly playing a part.

"You were great!" he said when he went out to meet her after the scene was finished. He was so enthusiastic that Holly had to quiet him down while another scene was being readied for final taping. She brought him to a quiet corner where they could talk.

"I finally picked up on the story line," he said proudly. "Lindsey didn't set out to get this rock star, Billy, but now that she knows her cousin is after him, she's intrigued by the competition, and she's in there pitching."

"I think you've managed to sum up about a month's worth of work in one minute," Holly whispered.

"That Aunt Lydia is something else! She's busy arranging a romance for Lindsey with some wealthy kid and doesn't give a darn what Lindsey wants." He tucked his finger under Holly's chin. "Poor kid—everybody manipulating you."

"Lindsey's not all that defenseless. She always takes care of herself. So how did you like the control room?"

"It's unbelievable. Here are all these people working at this frantic pace, and the moment the scene is over they pick up on conversations they had started before the frenzy began. Like the woman who does the split-second timing turns to the assistant director and says, 'So I said to the orthodontist, no braces. I mean, his teeth are *fine*.' " Tim was definitely hooked on the mechanics of producing a TV program.

"And remember, this goes on here four days a week—five one-hour segments to be filmed. I don't think I'll ever understand how it all comes together. But you can see why I love my job," Holly said, looking very pleased.

"I do. And I'll say it again, you're good at it. Can you show me the townhouse where Aunt Lydia lives?"

"Sure, but it's pretty dark now because they're filming on a set that's only about ten feet away." Tim looked confused. Holly took his arm and couldn't wait to see his expression when he saw the "townhouse."

"But it looks so big on the screen. And

where are the other three floors and the twenty rooms?"

Holly laughed. "The shot of the outside of the house is cut in. This is all there is to the parlor—three walls, and you have to be careful not to bump into them. They're as fragile as cardboard."

Tim walked to the stone mantel, touched it, and felt something like Styrofoam. "It's all so unreal," he said, lowering his voice. "But without the lights and the camera angles, we are two real people standing in what could be anyone's living room."

"It's just us," she said softly. "Only I have orange makeup on, and you don't." He held her shoulders gently and kissed her. Holly felt her body go limp. She was floating.

The overhead lights suddenly went on, burning down on the two of them. They broke apart to the applause of the cast on the next set.

"Now that's the way it should be done *on-camera*, too," Chris called over.

Holly flushed through her orange foundation, grabbed Tim's hand, and the two ran from the townhouse set.

Her workday was over, and it was still early. They were feeling giddy as they left the studio and stepped out into a bright and nippy November day.

Holly's instinct was to signal for a cab, but Tim reached out and took her arm before she could flag one down. "Let's walk to Penn Station. We'll still get a train and be back in time for your classes. I feel so supercharged after all I saw this morning, I think I need the walk to come back down to earth."

They started out quickly, zigzagging through the crowds. "You know," Tim said, "all the times I've been in Manhattan, I've never really walked around. I was always going to a museum or a zoo or a parade, but never doing what we're doing right now."

"Neither have I. I never thought about it until you mentioned it. For me it's been cabs for years, to and from the station." Holly looked up at Tim. Her own head barely reached the level of his shoulder.

"Then let's think of this as an adventure," he said, taking her hand at the corner and watching for the WALK sign to flash.

Holly felt like a tourist, taking in every sight and studying the passing faces.

"I think I just saw a mirage," she said. "Look over there!" Tim turned, and they both burst into laughter. Coming down the street was a hot dog vendor with his pushcart. Attached with leashes to the cart were four grace-ful greyhounds, walking sedately alongside.

"Early or not," Tim said, laughing, "we're buying a hot dog." He signaled to the vendor, who looked glad for the business. The wheels rolled to a stop, and the dogs sat in unison.

"The dogs—" Holly began.

"How many?" asked the cheerful vendor, who displayed two gold teeth in his broad grin.

"I mean *your* dogs," Holly said, giggling. "The *real* ones!"

"Oh, they're not for sale. These are my friends—my working companions during the long days."

Holly laughed. "I didn't want to *buy* them, but you've answered my question as to why they're with you."

"No hot dogs? You don't want any?" The man looked sad.

"Two," said Tim, "with everything on them."

"Gotcha!" The golden smile flashed again.

The remainder of their "walking adventure" maintained the same level of lighthearted fun often bordering on the zany. By the time they reached Penn Station, Holly's face hurt from laughing. They still had a few minutes before catching their train.

"I want to buy you something to remember this terrific morning." Tim looked around the station entrance for inspiration.

"That's it," he said, pointing to a sidewalk display of canvas hats, porkpie style with colorful bands. He pulled her along with him, grabbed one with a red band, and plopped it on Holly's head. As he paid the street vendor, Holly picked up a duplicate hat, fumbled in her bag for money, and crowned Tim.

"Now we do have to run," he said, breaking into a sprint, Holly trying to match his long stride. They ran into Penn Station, and Holly directed Tim to the right track.

"Do you think people are laughing at *us* now, dressed like twins?" She was almost out of breath.

"Not likely," he said when they finally reached the platform and slowed down. "Look over there," he said as they started to board the train.

Walking briskly down the platform was a man holding the skeleton of an umbrella over his head. Hanging from the spokes were glittering ornaments and trinkets that bobbed and danced as he walked. None of the other passersby took notice. Tim had to literally lift Holly onto the train, she was laughing so hard.

"My sides hurt from laughing," Tim said, collapsing on the seat next to Holly. "You should have seen your face when Umbrella Man walked by!"

"Tim, I don't think I can laugh any more! My cheekbones ache." They held hands and took time to regain their breath and composure. Neither spoke until the train broke from the pitch-black tunnel into golden daylight.

"This has been more exhausting than a full day at the studio, and I loved every minute of it." Holly sighed contentedly.

"I want to say something I hope *isn't* going to make you laugh." Tim leaned closer to her. "Remember that whole mess about the dance and Billy? I said I had no right to be angry, that you were a free agent. Well, it's not entirely true." He pulled his porkpie hat down over his face and said very quickly, "I want you to be my girl."

He lifted his hat enough to check her reaction. Her smile was widening. "You *are* going to laugh," he accused.

"Of course I am! I want to laugh because I'm so happy! I *want* to be your girl—very much."

He held her hand more tightly, and Holly

closed her eyes, hoping to make the precious moment last even longer. When she opened them, the train was passing the automated coffeepot. I will think of Tim every time I pass that sign, she said to herself.

Chapter Ten

The weatherman was predicting snow for Thanksgiving Day, but Andrea was predicting gloom. "No pun intended," she said on the cold morning walk to school, "but I think Thanksgiving this year is for the birds."

Holly had been wondering to herself just how much longer she would be able to wear her porkpie hat. Even that day it didn't offer much protection from the cold. She was also daydreaming about Tim but turned her attention to her friend. "Because your parents won't be together? Is that why you're down on the holiday?"

"This one and the next one that follows." An old weathered basketball on the path was the victim of Andrea's anger. She kicked it hard, watching it fly and then fall in a pile of brown leaves. "Now I feel better. Ever try kicking something when you're mad? It helps."

"Lately, I don't feel the need to kick anything. Remember our first weeks at Haycroft? I had doubts that I'd ever be part of the group. And now I'm accepted!"

"I still have my doubts," Andrea admitted.

"About me making friends?"

"No, about the friends you're making."

"Not again," Holly said with despair. "Didn't we begin a similar argument this way?"

"No argument. Just a friendly warning. I don't have all the evidence in yet, but I think you're being used."

"Ridiculous! Look at all the invitations we've had in the past few weeks."

"How many autographed pictures of Billy Gabriel have you provided lately?" Andrea countered.

Holly was picking up speed, trying to build her case. "What about Billy's rock concert?"

"That invitation, if you can call it that, came after you mentioned you could get discount tickets."

"OK. I give up! You win."

"It's not a game, just food for thought. I'm on a deep-thinking kick lately."

"What *I* think," Holly said in exhaustion, "is that you're preparing for a career as a lawyer."

Zipping her red jacket up to her chin, Holly did give some thought to Andrea's theory. But then a sudden wind caught the brim of her hat, blowing it off her head, and she ran to catch·it.

Something's missing, Holly said to herself as she walked from her final class that day. There was a cardboard turkey on the main bulletin board, but there didn't seem to be much preholiday excitement, the kind she'd always remembered in junior high. It's football, she thought. I always liked the banners across the front hall and the big game and the pep rally. But here I have more friends, and I'd rather sacrifice football cheers for them.

Hailey seemed to prove that point a second later. "Want to go shopping today?" she asked.

"Sure. What do you want to buy?"

"Nothing in particular. I thought we could just do some stores."

Funny, Holly thought, as she and Hailey walked to town, that none of the other girls were coming along. They usually traveled in a group. Holly almost asked Andrea to join them but remembered her friend was in the after-school gym program. Andrea was determined to conquer her fear of the uneven parallel bars.

Exploring the first two stores was fun, but Holly was getting bored just wandering up and down aisles, looking at counters and leafing through records she wouldn't allow herself to buy. With Christmas coming, she was saving for family presents and for something extraspecial for Tim. Almost all of the money she earned on the soap was put into the bank, so she had to save like everyone else.

"Maybe we should be starting back now," Holly suggested.

"Not yet. I'm having a good time. Aren't you?"

Holly was fed up with window shopping but didn't dare admit it. "Oh, yes," Holly said, doing her best Lindsey-type response.

Twenty minutes later when Hailey finally announced "Let's go," Holly was relieved. But instead of turning up Sherwood Road toward home, Hailey pulled Holly in the opposite direction.

"Just one more stop. I really should run into White's and pick up a bag of oranges my mother wants."

Tim would be there. Holly felt a sudden panic. She had never introduced any of her Haycroft friends to Tim, never mentioned that he was her boyfriend. Why, she wondered, did she want to keep the world she shared with Tim separate from the one at Haycroft? Was she afraid he might not approve of her new crowd?

No more time to think—they were at White's door. "I'll just stay up front here and leaf through some magazines. You go ahead and get the oranges. I'll meet you at the checkout counter," Holly said. Anything, she thought, to avoid the produce counter where Tim would be at the scales.

Seeing her own cover picture staring at her from the magazine rack, Holly grabbed another magazine and started flipping through the pages. What's taking her so long? Holly wondered. How long does it take to pick up a bag of oranges? I'll go and wait outside for her—no, I promised I'd meet her at the checkout, and she'll be mad if she has to come looking for me.

Hailey's blond, frizzy-permed head finally appeared at the counter, and Holly, much relieved, went over to her. The magazine with her picture was also at the checkout counter along with *TV Guide* and other last-minute items customers might be induced to buy while waiting in line.

"My friend here is the girl on the cover," Hailey was saying to an unknown woman in line behind her.

"Really," the woman said, trying to keep a squirming baby in the cart seat. "Why, it *is* you! I'll buy a copy if you sign it. My husband will be thrilled!"

Holly was about to hunt for a pen when she heard a voice behind them.

"I'll have to ask you both to empty your purses on the counter." It was the store manager. Holly didn't know his name, but she'd seen him many times.

"But—why? Is there a problem? What's going on?" Holly felt her skin become clammy.

"Please," the manager said, "let's not cause a scene over this."

Her fingers were numb as she turned her bag upside down and shook out a cascade of makeup, combs, wallet, key case, the works. The manager looked at her and then at what was spread out. "Fine. You can put all that back. You next," he said, indicating Hailey.

Hailey looked so casual that Holly felt confident they would be on their way in a minute, laughing about the episode all the way home.

Watching the brown saddle bag's contents tumble to the counter, Holly's throat constricted. She made no sound as she saw a necklace, earrings, and a scarf, all with the price tags still on. Holly had seen them less than thirty minutes before in MacHugh's department store.

"This is what I was looking for," the manager said as he held up an unopened plastic packet with a tube of lipstick inside. "You'd better step into my office. We can wait there for the police." He motioned Holly to come with them and then called over his shoulder, "Tim, would you come into the office for a moment?"

Holly hadn't even seen Tim. She couldn't feel her feet moving, yet in a moment she was down the aisle and sitting across from the manager with Hailey next to her. She looked up at Tim, and he gave her a reassuring smile. Her glance at Hailey was met with a cool shrug of the shoulders.

Try as she would, Holly couldn't concentrate on the conversation or focus on the faces around her. "Yes, police department . . . report a shoplifting. . . . She's here right now. . . . Other tags were MacHugh's. You might want to notify them . . . Right . . . wait for you here."

When the manager hung up the phone, Tim bent over the desk and whispered something to the man. He said something to Tim, then turned to Holly and asked her a question. "What?" she asked in a daze.

"Holly," Tim said. "He wants to be sure that you weren't covering for Hailey."

"Covering?"

"You know—acting as a decoy while someone else shoplifts."

Holly began to cry. Tim put his hand on her shoulder. "It's OK. I already told him that you were nowhere near the cosmetics display because *I* was near there, and I would have seen you. I—I told him you're my girl, and you'd never do anything like that."

Holly looked up at him, his image blurred by tears. The manager told her she could leave, and Holly stood, clutching her purse. Tim started after her but stopped when the manager asked him to return to work. Holly needed him now, and he felt helpless, watching her turn and run down the aisle.

Running from the store, Holly was vaguely aware of knocking down a display of paper towels but didn't stop until she was safe on the sidewalk in front of the store. As she took several deep breaths to gain some control, Holly looked up to see the woman who had asked for her autograph climbing into her car. The woman's stare was long, hard, and accusing.

What was the shortest route home? Holly wondered, again approaching panic. Which way? She turned to her left and began walking, then broke into a run when she reached Sherwood Road.

Chapter Eleven

"I heard what happened. Oh, darling, you must be so upset." Holly fell gratefully into her mother's arms and began to sob.

"It's going to be all right, honey." Her mother smoothed Holly's hair soothingly.

When Holly had calmed down, she told her mother the whole story. When she had finished, she asked, "How did you hear about it?"

"It's a grapevine kind of story—proves how fast it works in this town." She stopped a moment and went on. "Andrea's mother got a call from a friend whose daughter is a year ahead of you at Haycroft. She happened to be in the store and, well . . ." Her voice trailed off.

"Haycroft! It will be all over school tomorrow! I'll be so embarrassed!" Holly started to cry again. "Everyone will think I was part of the shoplifting, even if it isn't the truth. Oh, Mom," she said, taking comfort in her mother's arms, "I never want to go back to Haycroft again!"

"It's only natural to feel that way. You're very upset. What I want you to do is go on up and take a nice, long bath. Throw in some of my good oil and salts if you like. Then when your father comes home, we'll discuss all of this."

"But—"

"No buts. When you've relaxed, we'll all talk." Holly wearily mounted the stairs, like a toy robot whose batteries were running down.

In the bathroom she flung a round sponge into the tub and watched as the tub began to fill. I'll get a tutor, she thought. The studio will pay for one. They've always offered, but *I* wanted to go to a *regular* school—be just like other kids! Dreamer! With a firm twist, she shut off both taps.

Despite her tearful pleadings to her parents, they convinced her to face the girls at Haycroft and give it another try. She had nothing to be ashamed of. They said running away to HS and a tutor was an escape. And they both came down on her for what they called her irresponsible behavior since she had started school.

"It's as if you've been caught up in a whirlwind," her mother said, "rushing from one party or sleep-over to the next and not really enjoying yourself. It's almost as if you're afraid to say no to these girls."

Holly had no answer for her mother but thought about what she'd said. Was she really afraid that the girls would drop her if she didn't go along with all their plans? And what would happen now when she'd been connected with a shoplifting? I'll be back where I started, she thought, with only one friend. Holly felt she would be going to school the next day with the same trepidations she'd had on her first day of kindergarten.

If only I had a taping this morning, she wished as she headed for the assembly hall. She had deliberately dawdled on the way to school to avoid the usual morning conversations at the lockers. What stopped her short was seeing Amanda's signal to sit next to her.

Amanda patted the empty seat as an invitation, grinning all the while. She must have heard the news, but she's still my friend!

Holly smiled and walked quickly down to Amanda's row.

"Isn't it exciting?" Amanda gushed.

"What?" Holly put her books under her seat.

"You and Hailey and your caper yesterday." The other girls were leaning closer, straining to hear what was being said.

"What did you pick up?" Carley whispered.

"That's not important," Amanda snapped. "What we want to know is where you hid whatever you lifted. Confidentially, I think Hailey was a jerk for using her purse again. That's how she got caught last time. It's like she was looking to get pinched."

Holly looked confused. "Amanda, I didn't . . ." At that moment the national anthem was sounding, and the entire assembly got noisily to its feet.

Holly's thoughts were so muddled, she didn't hear the anthem stop. Amanda had to pull her back down into her seat. Holly also didn't hear a word of the program on the true meaning of Thanksgiving. They're actually excited about what happened yesterday, she thought. Anger began to replace her confusion. Hailey must be nuts, but they think she was stupid to get caught! What kind of friends are they, anyway? I can't tell them off now, but I'll give it to them at lunchtime.

By the time the assembly was over, Holly had mentally rehearsed what she would say to the group at the lunch table. As they started to rise, the headmistress called them back to order. "You may not all be aware that during early gym practice this morning, one of your classmates was injured. I will keep you posted as soon as we hear from the hospital any word of Andrea Gelfand."

"Andrea!" Holly shouted. Turning angrily to Amanda, she said, "You *knew* about this?"

"Yeah—we heard the ambulance arrive. I didn't see the accident."

"She's my best friend," Holly cried and pushed through the crowd of girls, then ran out of the assembly hall.

The last words she heard were Carley's. "What's got her so uptight?"

"Mother? I'm at the hospital. No, no, I'm fine. It's Andrea. She fell from the uneven parallel bars, and I'm here with her mother waiting to see how she is. . . . No, I didn't ask permission to leave school grounds. . . . Mother, I don't care if you call Haycroft or not. . . . Yes . . . yes. I'll let you know as soon as I know, and I'll give her your love." Holly replaced the receiver of the pay phone. She fought back the tears that might upset Mrs. Gelfand, but she couldn't make the sinking feeling in her stomach disappear, not until she knew Andrea was going to be all right.

Mrs. Gelfand paced the emergency waiting area. It was empty except for her and Holly, who sat stiffly in one of the blue plastic chairs. It was uncomfortable, but Holly felt too dizzy to stand. Her head was spinning with all that had happened in the past two days. Holly felt overcome with remorse, thinking how she'd neglected Andrea. Her friend was going through so much with her parents' divorce, and instead of helping her, Holly had been out to win a popularity contest. And for what? For a bunch of girls who thought stealing was cool. Andrea was right—they'd probably been using her all along. They'd never really liked her for herself, but for what she could do for them.

"Mrs. Gelfand?" The tall, graying doctor had been gone for hours, it seemed. Mrs. Gelfand turned to him, and Holly jumped from her chair.

"You can both stop looking so grim. Andrea's a lucky girl."

"You mean she's all right? Oh, thank goodness! I've been so frightened ever since I got that phone call from the school. I—I . . ." Mrs. Gelfand was unable to finish her sentence. She broke into sobs of relief, the first she had allowed herself. She hugged Holly, who shared her joy.

"As I said," the doctor continued, "she has no serious injury, but the fall was a shock to her spinal column, and she is in some pain from the muscle spasms that resulted." He sensed Mrs. Gelfand's concern and reassured her.

"I've given her something for the pain, but I don't think she should go home today. We'll keep her here overnight. She may feel some stiffness for a few days, but again, that will go away."

"May I see her now?" Mrs. Gelfand asked.

"Yes, and after that, I will allow her anxious friend here a short visit." He smiled at Holly and placed a hand on her shoulder.

More waiting, but this time Holly didn't mind. She knew Andrea would recover. She hoped she'd never see that waiting room again!

Mrs. Gelfand finally returned looking happy and said, "You can go in now, Holly. I'm going to go home, get some of her things for the night, and call her father. It was so kind of you to stay with me. It means so much to know what a good friend Andrea has in you." She gave Holly a hug.

I should have been a better friend, Holly thought as she opened the door to Andrea's room. The sight of Andrea in that setting, wearing a neck brace and draped in white, unnerved her. Suddenly Holly felt awkward, unsure of what to say.

Andrea looked up at Holly and smiled wryly. "This is what *you'd* call A-number-one stupid. I thought I knew what I was doing, but obviously I didn't. So how do you like my necklace?"

Holly flinched at the word "necklace." It reminded her of the escapade the day before. "Wrong choice of word, I guess, after what you just went through," Andrea said. They both started to laugh, though Andrea winced at the pain.

"Stop laughing or you'll be in here more than just one night," Holly warned her.

"You know, I wanted to call you last night after I heard what happened at White's, but I was afraid I'd say something wrong. Today was when I planned to talk to you. But then I was attacked by these two uneven parallel bars and—well, you know the rest."

"You *should* have phoned and called me every name you could think of!" Holly could feel the tears welling up. "You were right about that group. All those questions you asked me the other day—now I understand." She went on to tell Andrea what had happened at assembly that morning, including the part about the girls deliberately not mentioning the accident.

"You're not the only one acting like an idiot lately. I've let my parents' problems become *mine*. All it accomplished was to make me angry at the world." Andrea's face showed the pain, both physical and mental, that she was suffering. "This morning changed all that. I mean, when you can't move and you're afraid you may never be able to walk again, it's really mind-blowing."

"Is that why you signed up for the after-school gym programs and the early-morning practice sessions—to work off your anger?" Holly asked.

"That, and to prove to myself I could conquer the bars and my fear of tossing myself into space. Now I couldn't care less about any of it. Being able to perform on the uneven parallel bars is not the most useful accomplishment in the world, you know?" They both laughed.

"I get the idea." Holly was serious again. "The same message applies to me and what

I've been doing. Problem is, what are we going to do to turn things around for both of us—me and Haycroft and you and your parents?"

"I'm not making any grand plan, that's for sure! But first thing I'm going to do is tell my folks that I don't want one Thanksgiving dinner in Amsbly and one in Manhattan. I want to be here for the whole weekend. I want to bake a pumpkin pie from scratch, sleep in my own bed for the first Saturday in months, and be with my friends."

Holly squeezed Andrea's hand to let her know she understood. "First thing *I'm* going to do after I get back from the studio tomorrow is to tell off Amanda and her crowd. And after school I'm going to White's and buy you a get-well present of—a bag of avocados!"

Chapter Twelve

There was a new twist brewing in the plot. Holly studied the blackboard for the current and upcoming HS story line. It looked like a drawing of a family tree. She could locate herself instantly. Under Aunt Lydia were lines and boxes. Two more rows of lines and boxes under those listed Lindsey and Sheila as grandnieces. One of them was slated for on-location filming. On location could mean anything from a local street scene to a trip to Hong Kong! Holly raced to the office of the executive producer.

Executive producer Frank Gillen was the only man, cast and crew included, who came to work in a suit and tie. He looked up from his paperwork when Holly walked into the room.

"Frank, I just saw the master plan and a possible on-location!" The excitement in her voice made him smile. His usual look was that of a serious banker considering a loan application from a panhandler.

"On location? Yes. Trinidad. Whether Lindsey or Sheila makes the trip hasn't been decided." Frank was a man of few words.

"When *will* it be decided?"

"Up to you."

"It's up to me?" She felt near shock. "But why?"

"Story can go either way. One niece goes with Lydia for a vacation in Trinidad. The one who stays behind makes a play for Jed Shine. Either way, story line follows the same. Get the picture?"

"Got it." Now she had adopted his pattern of speech. "But why *my* decision?"

"Seniority," he told her. "You've been on the show three years. What's-her-name—Sheila—has only been with us a year and a half. So it's your choice."

Holly swallowed hard. She could hardly believe her ears.

"The trip to Trinidad would be kind of a reward—a feather in your TV cap," Frank continued, explaining that the scenes in Trinidad would draw a bigger audience. Depending on viewer response, a larger part in the show for Holly could be in the offing.

Any moment she knew she would wake up from this dream. "I've got to pinch myself. This isn't real," she said and sighed.

"It's real, all right. But don't wait too long to make your decision. Talk it over with your parents. Don't leave us hanging too long. The shooting would be over the Christmas holidays, so you wouldn't miss school."

"I'll let you know as soon as I can. And Frank—" He had already returned to his paperwork. "Thank you. Thank you very much!" On impulse she bent and kissed his cheek.

"Go on, get out of here," he said good-naturedly. "No need to get all sloppy about it."

Elated at the prospect of a trip to Trinidad, Holly gave one of her best performances that morning. Lindsey for the first time had the courage to stand up to Aunt Lydia. She delivered her last line with such force that the actress who played Lydia reacted with true surprise.

LINDSEY: [*Angry.*] Just stop trying to run my life the way you have with everyone else in this family. And as for your threat, you can take my inheritance, cut it up, and tuck it in your teabags!

[*Take* LYDIA *stunned. Fade.*]

After Chris announced the scene was "in the can," he called to Holly. "Have to get more angry scenes for you. You had some recent practice lately in getting mad?"

Holly just smiled. There'd be lots more practice, she knew, when she got back to Haycroft.

It amazed Holly that she could feel so hungry knowing that once she selected her lunch, she would be joining Amanda and Company for a showdown. The spaghetti looked tempting, but she took a chicken salad sandwich instead. It would be just her luck, she thought, to tell them all off with tomato sauce dripping down her chin.

"So, what happened to you yesterday?" Carley asked. "You ran out of assembly like the hall was on fire!"

"My best friend had been hurt," Holly said quietly and took a bite from the corner of her sandwich. There was no response from Carley.

Amanda took the opportunity to bring up the subject she most wanted to hear about. "Can we get back to where we were when you ran out? You shouted at me, by the way, and

I don't like that from my friends." She paused, waiting for an apology from Holly, but it didn't come.

She went on anyway. "How did you hide what you lifted the other day?"

Holly drew on the straw in her milk container. The others were getting impatient. "How is Hailey? Where is she now?" she asked.

"Oh, they let her go," someone answered. "Her father knows the police chief."

"Will she have to go to court?" Holly drank more milk and took another bite.

"Court?" They all laughed.

"With *her* father?"

"She was out in half an hour this time, with another warning."

"Hailey gets to stay home till after the holiday. Suspended again."

"Lucky! Gives her more time to finish her term paper."

Amanda was back in charge of the conversation. "So, answer what I've already asked you twice. Fill us in," she commanded.

Holly had finished her sandwich and blotted her mouth with her napkin, which she rolled up and shoved in the empty milk container.

"OK. I'll fill you in," she said, looking at the eager faces. "I didn't know Hailey was shoplifting. I have never taken anything in my life—I take that back. I found a gumball in a machine one day that someone forgot. I chewed it, but I felt guilty all day."

The faces of her audience were beginning to freeze. "I was scared that afternoon when the manager asked us to dump our bags—not exhilarated, as you believed. I wanted to get out of there as fast as I could, but first I had to prove that I wasn't covering for Hailey.

"I couldn't do that, but Tim Hartley could. He's a clerk at White's, and he's also my boyfriend. He'd been watching me, and he swore I didn't take anything." She felt proud hearing her own voice pronounce Tim her boyfriend.

"You creep! You led Hailey to believe you were one of us and then let her take the blame all by herself!" Amanda's rage was felt throughout the dining hall. "And a grocery clerk! Your boyfriend? When you could have had Billy Gabriel? You're sick!"

Holly stood and gathered up her lunch debris. "No, *Hailey* is sick and needs help. As for the rest of you, what you do with your lives is *your* problem, not mine." She turned away, walked to the nearest trash can, and

119

emptied her tray. It was peace, not anger, she felt as she left the room.

When the school day was finally over, it was sheer joy for Holly to find Tim waiting for her outside the main building. She didn't care who was watching as she ran to his welcoming arms.

"I've been worried about you," he said. "Come on. Let's get out of here and talk."

Holly held his hand tightly as they walked. Tim told her that he had called her the day of the shoplifting, but her mother had said she was in the bathtub. "She said you were too upset to speak to anyone. And yesterday I heard about Andrea's accident. I wanted to go over to your house right after work, but I didn't know if that was the right thing to do," he said.

"Next time, trust your instincts! But you know, over the past couple of days I think I've started to get my head together," she said and tightened her grip on his hand.

"Well, you look great. In fact, compared to the last time I saw you, you look completely together—beautifully together."

Holly filled him in on all that had gone on at school with Amanda's crowd, and then it was Tim's turn to talk. He had not only planned a full holiday weekend—pep rally, football game, and victory—or loser—dance, but he wondered if Andrea would be interested in a blind date with his friend, Todd, whose girlfriend had just broken up with him.

Holly beamed. "I'm sure she would!" It was going to be the best Thanksgiving ever, she just knew it.

Chapter Thirteen

Holly was glad her mother had invited Andrea and Mrs. Gelfand for Thanksgiving dinner. It gave Andrea a sense of family, Holly could tell. Everyone was in high spirits, even though dinner had some hitches—such as Andrea's pumpkin pie. She'd used all the proper ingredients and followed the recipe, but for some reason the filling didn't gel. They all ate it with spoons and heaped praise on Andrea. And Holly's father insisted that he had sharpened the carving knife, yet the turkey was served in chunks, not slices. Mrs. Giles didn't remember to serve the extra chestnut stuffing until the dinner was nearly over and everyone was already stuffed.

Part of the girls' happiness had to do with Tim and his friend Todd. The four had gone to the pep rally and bonfire the night before, and earlier that day they had attended the Amsbly-Milford football game. As Holly began to clear the table, she thought about the game. What stuck in her mind was the warm reception from Tim's friends. And Andrea and Todd seemed a perfect match.

Stacking the plates in the dishwasher, Holly smiled, remembering the fun she'd had that afternoon. She'd cheered herself hoarse, and in the final minutes of the game, she was jumping up and down, screaming for a touchdown. Amsbly won. But what was best was Tim hugging and kissing her at the moment of victory. And the next night was the dance—even more fun to look forward to.

"That pie was the pits," Andrea said, laughing and holding the pie plate containing the soggy remains. "Honestly, I don't know if we should wrap the rest or pour it in a soup bowl!"

"How did you like the turkey chunks? Poor Dad! No one dared to laugh. He does the same thing every year, but it was more fun having someone to suffer with."

"I wouldn't have cared if your mother had forgotten the turkey instead of the stuffing. It was just so good to be part of it all. For Mom, too—took our minds off past holiday dinners." Andrea looked thoughtful but not sad.

"Where is everyone?" Holly asked as she took the pie from Andrea.

"In the living room. Well, actually, your dad's out getting more wood for the fire, and our mothers are discussing women returning to work—the new marketplace, they call it. That's when I offered to come out and help you."

"I'm glad you did. Listen—remember we were all talking at dinner about my going to Trinidad?"

"How could I forget? You said there was no way I could pass myself off as the wardrobe mistress and tag along," Andrea teased.

"I'd really appreciate it if you didn't mention anything to Tim about it right away. I haven't told him yet, and I'm kind of waiting for a—well, you know—private moment."

"I get it. Moonlight and roses and stuff like that."

"I just want to make sure things don't get fouled up the way they did about the Halloween dance. This is one secret that I'm going to share with him myself."

"OK. I won't say anything if *you* won't tell a soul that I really like Todd. I can hardly wait for the dance tomorrow night!" Andrea flipped the start button on the dishwasher. "Boy, am I glad I'm staying over with you after the dance. For the first time we'll have something new to talk about. Boys!"

"Two *special* boys," Holly whispered conspiratorially. Giggling, they went to join the others in the living room.

"Dancing is OK if you know how," Tim proclaimed to Holly as they entered the decorated gym the next night at Amsbly High.

"Well, do you?" She looked up at him affectionately. He looked so handsome in a suit and tie. The reason for the "formal" dress, he had explained, was tradition. Team wins, you dress up for the dance. Team loses, it's jeans and sweatshirts. Holly was wearing the rust velvet, once again on loan from wardrobe, and Tim was properly impressed.

"Question is, do *you*?"

"Well, I guess so. We've had to do dance scenes on HS—disco, rock, new wave, and that sort of thing."

"That answers my question. You lead, except for the slow dances."

"Deal," she said as he took her arm. The five-piece band was warming up, testing amplifiers and electric keyboard.

To the disco beat, Tim let her lead. Others began to follow Holly and were learning new steps. Andrea and Todd seemed to be looking only at each other.

"Now it's my turn to lead," Tim said as the soft strains of a slow number began. The band was playing Billy's "What Can I Do?" They exchanged knowing smiles as the first bars were played. They swayed gently together, Holly tuned in to his every move. He may not have qualified as a super dancer, but all she cared about was that he was dancing with her.

During breaks they talked with the other kids. They asked her questions about HS and told her they tried to watch her on it when it didn't conflict with after-school activities. But most of the talk was about sports, teachers, and the pre-Christmas excitement.

"My friends all like you," Tim said as they drove to her home.

"They really do?" asked Holly hopefully.

"Does that surprise you?"

"A little, I guess."

"It shouldn't," he said firmly. "Oh, sure, they were excited about your being on a soap, but they're just as excited when a boy or girl wins a gold letter in sports. Holly, they liked you because you're you!" He reached over at a stoplight and squeezed her hand.

This is the right moment, she said to herself, to tell him the good news about Trinidad. But Tim was already off on a new subject.

"I've got so many plans for us at Christmastime. It's all the kind of stuff that's been going on for years—the ice carnival, the Snow Ball, the evening sleigh ride, the skating party." He stopped to swallow. "But this is the first time I've really wanted to do all that stuff because—because I'll be doing it with you."

Holly saw his smile as he studied the road and navigated the sharp turn into her driveway. She decided at that moment to wait until the HS schedule for Trinidad was finalized before telling him about it. Maybe she could do all he had planned for them and still make the trip. There was no sense spoiling that wonderful feeling. And then Tim stopped the car, and his kiss drove every other thought from her mind.

"Andrea, are you asleep?" In her darkened bedroom Holly could barely see the outline of her friend's head in the next bed.

"No, but I thought we were all talked out."
They'd had a nonstop conversation since returning from the dance, jumping from one subject to another and always coming back to Tim or Todd. Andrea was glowing because Todd had asked her for another date.

Holly propped herself up on one elbow but didn't turn on the light. "What are we going to do?"

"About what?" Andrea yawned.

"About Haycroft."

"I've been thinking about that a lot." She was more awake now and turned toward Holly's voice.

"I remember what you said in the hospital that day about taking on one problem at a time. And I think the time has come to make a decision."

"I know what you mean. This weekend had something to do with it—for me, anyway."

"Me, too," Holly added. "I know now that I don't want to go back to Haycroft. And it's not to escape like I wanted to do after the mess with Hailey. What I want is the good feeling I had this weekend with the kids at Amsbly. Even the ones who gave me a hard time in junior high were really nice."

Andrea sat up. "I felt the same. At first I thought it was just being thrilled over Todd, but it's more than that. I was comfortable being with the Amsbly kids. I could almost picture myself going to classes there. And did you get a look at the bulletin board outside the gym? There's so much going on! I think the first thing I'd do is join the school newspaper."

"How do we tell our parents?"

"Can you imagine me telling my father that I don't want his gift of a fancy private-school education?" Andrea winced at the prospect.

"And my parents, who thought the smaller classes at Haycroft would offer a better chance for learning. I know they're right—it *is* a good school academically." Holly turned on her back. "So we're back to my original question. What do we do?"

"For now, we do what my grandmother always said. Sleep on it."

With that they fell silent, but Holly sensed from Andrea's breathing that she stayed awake thinking for a long time afterward. Holly herself didn't close her eyes until almost dawn, mulling over the trip to Trinidad, her feelings for Tim, and her desire to change schools. As she finally felt drowsiness overcome her, her last thought was that Andrea's grandmother obviously didn't have many problems to resolve when she'd advised Andrea to "sleep on it."

Chapter Fourteen

"Figure five million watching HS right now. Take the Trinidad segments, add more kids home and watching during the week after the holiday, and I say we double the audience." The executive producer Frank Gillen looked more haggard than Holly had ever seen him. Even his tie was slightly askew.

She waited in his doorway until he finished his meeting with the associate producer and directors. Press representative Shawn Mullen was also there taking notes. "We can get top promotion on this," Shawn said. "If we shoot on schedule, we can slip promo slots into every afternoon network soap the week before. I may even be able to get *Teen Fashion* magazine to do a piece on the beach and resort clothes the grandniece will be wear-

131

ing for the scenes. Question is, *which* niece do you plan the wardrobe for?"

Frank spotted Holly. "Come on in. Have a schedule here and an itinerary. Take it home, look it over, and let me know."

"I will, Frank, as soon as possible." Holly couldn't wait to get her hands on the schedule.

"Tomorrow," he said.

She faltered but assured him, "Tomorrow."

As she walked back to her dressing room, Holly tried to read the schedule, and she ran smack into Billy.

"Hey, watch it," he teased. "You could get a ticket for a moving violation."

"Sorry, Billy. It's the schedule for the Trinidad scenes. I've got to look it over."

"So you've decided to go. Great break, and you deserve it. I'll miss you while you're away. You're easier to work with than Karen." Karen was the girl who played Sheila, and being a relatively recent addition to the cast, she usually messed up the pacing on a scene.

"That's nice of you to say, Billy, but I haven't made my final decision. I've got to fit this schedule into another and . . ."

"Must be something pretty important for you to even think about passing up Trinidad. Look, I'm kind of new to this business to be giving advice, but this is a big chance for you, especially if you're planning a future as an actress."

Holly considered what he said. "You're right. Somehow, I'll fit everything together. Thanks for caring enough to talk to me the way you just did."

"You can thank me by jumping in a cool blue pool in sunny Trinidad while I'm up here beating a blizzard to work." He went off, humming a tune Holly had never heard.

Her first chance to study the schedule carefully was on the train heading home. Now she knew when she would leave for Trinidad and how long she would be there. What she had to do was find out the dates of the holiday events in Amsbly. Holly began dreaming about an evening sleigh ride with Tim. Then she saw the tip of the coffeepot and closed her eyes, recreating Tim's first kiss.

At Haycroft later, she found Andrea in the library. There were two encyclopedias spread before her, but Andrea was looking out the window at an early snowfall.

"Hi! It looks beautiful, doesn't it?" Holly said, indicating the nickle-size flakes dropping outside.

"What are you doing in here? I thought you'd be in English by now."

"Got a pass. I've only got a few minutes.

Listen, remember all the holiday plans I told you Tim was making? Do you know when they are? I mean, the dates for the ice carnival and all that?"

"Yeah, but what's—?"

"Just jot them down." Andrea, puzzled, scribbled the dates as best she could remember.

"Thanks. I'll explain later." Holly took the paper from Andrea, started out, then stopped. "Did you talk to your parents yet about transferring to Amsbly?"

"No. Dad's coming up this weekend, and I thought I'd wait to talk to them both at once. After all, they're still my parents, and this would have to be a mutual decision. What about you?"

"Not yet, but soon. I think I'm working on a crushing headache."

"Talk to you later," Andrea said, then added sympathetically, "Hang in there."

"You, too."

During English the class was discussing *Ethan Frome*, but Holly was distracted. Mrs. Nearing was asking something about symbolism and a sled. At the mention of the word "sled," Holly thought of the two schedules in her bag.

She removed Andrea's note and the studio schedule and slid them under the novel.

As Mrs. Nearing turned to write on the board, Holly quickly removed the book and studied the dates. There were conflicts! Only the ice carnival would be going on the week after she returned. No sleigh ride, no Winter Ball.

Depression and a slight headache hit her at once. How can I tell Tim? she wondered. What if he met someone else while she was away? Other thoughts were passing before her until her head was pounding. She knew she would have to find a way to tell her parents that she wanted to transfer to Amsbly, but she was afraid that they'd see it as giving up. All at once the room seemed stifling. Holly raised her hand and asked to be excused. In the empty restroom, she began to sob.

Tim met her after school and said he wished there was enough snow to have a snowball fight. At that point the snow was just beginning to stick. Walking in the snow is another "first" with Tim that I'll never forget, Holly thought. But she looked sad rather than cheerful.

"I wish I didn't have to go to work today," Tim said. "I'd like to keep walking, then take you to my house and have my mother make us hot chocolate with lots of marshmallows."

"I thought your mother was working?"

"She is. I just said that's what I'd *like* to do."

He always seemed to know what to say to make her smile. But Holly's smile quickly faded. Out with it, you coward, she told herself. "Tim, something's come up on HS."

"Lydia's cut you out of her will?"

"Be serious for one second! Over the Christmas vacation there's going to be more filming than I expected. And—"

"No problem. I'll even be able to drive you into the city. If I promise to drive my mother to and from work, I'll have the car the whole vacation." He tilted his head back and let the snow fall on his face, blinking when the flakes hit his eyes. He was on such a natural high, Holly hated to bring him down.

She tugged at his sleeve and made him look at her. "No! Let me finish. The filming *isn't* in the city. It's in Trinidad." His smile was gone.

Tim thrust his hands into his pockets and turned away, trying to collect himself. "That's great for you," he said and turned back to her again, trying as hard as he could to hide his true feelings. "I know how important this can be for your career. I—I guess I'd do the same. Not that Mr. White will ever

136

send me anywhere except to the storeroom." He tried to laugh at his own weak joke.

Holly didn't laugh that time. "I should feel happy that you understand. And I'm glad you do. But why isn't this girl smiling?"

"Come on," he said. "Race you across *our* Hartley Square!" He ran faster than she had ever seen him since they had started inventing silly races with no finish lines. He was nearly out of her sight by the time he stopped.

Chapter Fifteen

Trinidad, West Indies, is an island off the coast of Venezuela. Holly was at home, curled up in the blue tapestry wing chair, reading a travel booklet. The thought of being that close to South America made her shiver. A whole continent away, she said to herself, and pulled an afghan more tightly around her shoulders.

She skimmed over statistics on population and square miles until she found "climate." *Hot and humid . . . main shopping artery is Frederick Street. . . . Crops include sugarcane, limes, grapefruits . . .*

Tim! I read about grapefruits and produce, and I think of Tim. The booklet flew through the air and landed on the coffee table.

"So, what have you learned about Trinidad?" her mother asked.

"Grapefruit. Miles of grapefruit," Holly replied without thinking.

"I'm over here thinking about the exotic Port of Spain, and you say 'grapefruit.' It must be genetic. Your father does the same sort of thing every now and then. Says something that makes absolutely no sense at all."

"It's cold in here," Holly said, sinking deeper into the warmth of the afghan.

"You're wrapped up, you're sitting next to the fire, and the heat's up to seventy. You're not coming down with something, are you?"

"No—I was just thinking of how far away I'll be going, and I suddenly felt very cold."

"That's just pretravel jitters. Your father and I are experiencing some of the same symptoms, only ours are caused by knowing how much we'll miss you. It'll be the first time you haven't been home for the whole Christmas holiday."

"I'll miss you both, too." There was a sadness in her voice, and her mother detected it.

"Let's think of what an exciting adventure it will be for you. It's a learning experience for one thing, and a vacation for another."

Her mother went on talking about the

island and its history. The last Holly heard before retreating deep into her own thoughts was something about an asphalt lake almost two miles wide.

I won't be missing Christmas altogether, she tried to convince herself. The tree will be up long before I leave, and it will be here when I get back. The snow will be around for months after! I'll have a super tan. But the caroling—*that's* what I wanted to do with Tim for the first time. She had even bought matching mufflers to wear as an early Christmas present.

"What's this about Columbus?" Holly's father's voice cut short her daydreaming.

"Hi, dear. I was telling Holly that Columbus discovered Trinidad in 1498."

"Ah, yes," he said, doing a little spin as he walked across the room. "Native music and tropical forests. Olé!"

"Dear, I don't think they say 'olé' in the West Indies; English is the official language." Mrs. Giles laughed and looked at Holly, who wasn't joining in.

"It's off," she suddenly said to her parents.

"What? My singing or dancing?" her father quipped.

"Everything," she blurted out and threw off the afghan. "Trinidad and Haycroft. It's *all* off. I'm not going to Trinidad—I'll tell Frank tomorrow. And I'm not going to Haycroft next semester. I want to go to Amsbly."

The room was suddenly so quiet that even the fire seemed to have stopped crackling. Holly didn't know what was to come from her parents, but she felt an enormous sense of relief. She was now calm enough to defend her decision if necessary.

Her outburst was countered with a softly spoken question. "Why?"

"I'll have to tell it my way—one thing at a time." Her parents both nodded. By now her father was seated next to her mother. Holly walked over to the fire.

"First, about school." Her voice cracked, and she cleared her throat. "I've made some mistakes at Haycroft. I finally got a shooting schedule to fit my school schedule that would give me more time to make friends and be a part of school activities. What I did, though, was make time for the wrong kind of kids. I know there are lots of good kids at Haycroft and that I could try again, but the school just doesn't have all that I want. I miss the team sports and school spirit of a big high school. And cheerleading—I miss that, too. I don't even know if I'd be good enough to make the Amsbly squad, but I'd like to try." Holly stopped, hoping to read some reaction in her parents' expressions.

"Honey," her father said, "your mother and I have not been happy with what's been happening to you lately. You seemed to have had your values mixed up for a while, and we were hoping you'd figure that out on your own. It seems you have, and what you've just said makes good sense. I say go with the transfer." He looked at his wife.

"It's fine with me, Holly, as long as you realize that there isn't one perfect school. You'll have to cope with different problems every year of high school, just like all the other kids."

"I understand," she said and smiled, "but I may need you to repeat that a lot over the next few years."

"I'll make a tape." Her mother grinned.

Holly could hardly believe that they had agreed so easily. "You mean you don't mind? It's all right with you if I go to Amsbly High?"

"Honey, your mother and I have been discussing this possibility for weeks—ever since you started pulling your Lindsey routine around here," said her father. "I told you before, Holly Giles is the daughter I love. I want her back. If she wants to go to Amsbly, I'm all for it! But I'm a bit confused. If this matter is settled, why not go and enjoy the trip to Trinidad?" Her father waited for Holly, who was trying to choose her words.

"This is tough to explain. It has to do with Christmas, I guess. It's always been my favorite holiday. But this year it should be even better. For the first time I could be a part of a whole new scene with kids I really like. There's so much to do right here in Amsbly, and I want to find out what it's like to be a part of it all!"

"Does Tim have something to do with your decision?" her mother asked.

"Yes, in a way. But it was *my* decision. He never asked me *not* to go to Trinidad. He even said he was happy for me."

"I wasn't criticizing Tim, Holly. I'm glad you have Tim and his friends at this point in your life. I'll even go as far as to say, it's about time." Her mother looked to her father. "Oh, don't look so shocked, Jeff. Little girls *do* grow up."

"I guess they do. Come here, honey." He pulled Holly down next to him and gave her a hug. "You'll still have to work during the holidays, though, won't you?"

"Yes, but it will be mornings as always. And that should be fun, too. I'll get to do more scenes with Billy, and we've been working well together."

Holly's mother sighed. "Deep down, I'm glad you're not going to Trinidad. I would have been awake nights worrying about your being lost in a forest or burning up on an asphalt lake—or malaria—" She had to stop. She couldn't hear her own voice over the laughter next to her.

"Mom, you never change! *Malaria?*"

"It's not funny! A mother worries. Now both of you come give me a hand in the kitchen."

"May I make a quick phone call first?" Holly couldn't wait to call Andrea with her news. Tim wouldn't be home from work yet, and she was bursting to tell someone.

The foyer phone was nearest, and she dialed Andrea's number. It rang three times before she heard Andrea's voice.

"Hi, it's me! I have to talk to you."

"Can't right now. My dad's just leaving. I'll call you right back."

That's strange, Holly thought. She wasn't supposed to see her father till the weekend! Come on, Andrea, call back! Almost on cue the phone rang, and Holly grabbed it on a half ring.

"Andrea?"

"Yeah—and guess what?" There was more excitement than mystery in her voice. "I'm transferring to Amsbly!"

"So am I!" Holly said and squealed. "How come your dad came today? I thought—"

"Couldn't *stand* it! After you left the library, I decided that I shouldn't always have to wait for weekends to get some answers to my problems. Anyway, Dad came, and he and Mom agreed on the transfer. Mom said she didn't like the gym program after what happened to me, and Dad said I always looked tired when he saw me. Whatever the reasoning, I don't care. I'll make it at Amsbly!"

"I'm so happy for you and for me! Mom says high school is going to be a time of problems wherever I go, but frankly, I'd rather face them at Amsbly." Holly also shared her decision about staying around for the holidays and foregoing the trip to Trinidad.

"Have you told Tim yet?" Andrea asked.

"No, I'll call him later. Right now, I've got to help with dinner and then eat it! I'll talk to you tomorrow."

"OK." Andrea was about to hang up. Then, "Hey, Holly. You still there?"

"Just barely," she said, laughing.

"I just wanted to say—I feel like it's Christmas already!"

"Me, too. See ya." Holly hung up and stomped her heels on the slate floor. "Olé!"

Chapter Sixteen

"You told me once to trust my instincts. So here I am." Tim stood in Holly's doorway in the light of the carriage lamp.

Holly was surprised to see him, and to see that the snow was falling harder and sticking to the front steps. "I was going to call you when we finished dinner! It must be ESP."

"No, it must be bad timing if I'm interrupting your dinner."

"We've finished—except dessert, which I don't want because I'm too excited to eat."

"Something to do with Trinidad, I bet."

"Something," she said, smiling.

"Well, can the offer of a walk in the snow compete with Trinidad?"

Her smile was his answer. "Let me get my jacket and tell my parents we're going for a walk. I'll be right back." She started to close the door, then opened it again. "What am I doing? You don't have to stand out there. Come on in."

When she returned, she was wearing her new blue ski jacket and a red stocking cap.

"I've always liked you in red, ever since that morning on the train station. You're my Holly-berry," said Tim.

Holly felt the cold flakes hit her cheeks. The lawn she had watched her father rake just weeks before was white. Little chips of jewels glowed where the lights hit the snow.

"How do you feel about caroling at Christmastime?" she asked.

"It seems the most appropriate time of year to carol."

She grabbed some snow and flung it at him, missing by a foot. "I mean how do you feel about singing? And you *know* what I meant!"

"Same as dancing," he said in an authoritative tone. "It's OK if you know how."

"Then *learn* if you can't! I want to carol this year with you."

"And how do you plan to do that? Tape recording from Trinidad?"

"No. In person." She couldn't keep it up much longer. "I'm not going to Trinidad!"

Tim leaped into the air. He scooped up big handfuls of snow and flung them over his head as Holly stood there, laughing at his antics.

He looked embarrassed when he faced her and brushed the snow from his hands. "I guess I'm supposed to say I'm sorry your trip got canceled. Stupid of me, Holly. I know you must be disappointed."

"Tim, *I'm* the one who canceled the trip."

"But—"

"I made two decisions today. One was that I wanted to transfer to Amsbly High next semester, and the other was that I was going to spend the holidays here in Amsbly."

For once he was speechless. "Well, *say* something!" Holly pleaded.

"I—you've hit me with two things at once. I want to hug you and shout and race . . ." He stopped. "I have to know your reasons first. Did you make these decisions because of me? Because if you did, you shouldn't. You have your career to think about, and Haycroft isn't the worst—"

"Stop! Please!" Holly told him, as she had her parents, why she wanted to switch from Haycroft. "As for Trinidad, I'm sick of thinking of my career. I love my work, but I'm not ready to commit my life to it. I'd rather keep my part in HS just as it is for now."

Tim encircled her with his arms. "What I didn't tell my parents was that I wanted to be part of whatever you're doing this season," she said. "But I think they figured that out themselves."

"Will I be able to drive you to the studio then for your filming? You'll still have to work, won't you?"

"Of course. The part goes on—HS goes on, and Lindsey is going to try her best to get Jed Shine to be her boyfriend while Sheila is away. It'll all be in the script."

"So there's going to be time for ice skating?"

"And the ice carnival!"

"The Winter Ball." He laughed.

"I've got a red dress," Holly told him.

"And the sleigh ride?" He looked into her eyes.

"*Especially* the sleigh ride!" she answered breathlessly.

He kissed her and brushed the snow-flakes from her nose. "Race you to anywhere!" he said and took a head start.

Holly ran after him, laughing and slipping in the snow. As she ran she could have sworn she heard sleigh bells.

☐ **#54 I CAN'T FORGET YOU by Lois I. Fisher (On sale December 15, 1983 • 23940-6 • $1.95)**
—When Jeri and Kemp went out together last year, they were always going to movies, parties, dances—it was wonderful. But when her grades began to slide, Jeri had to choose her schoolwork over Kemp. For a while, she was sure she'd done the right thing. Her grades went up, and then she met serious, sensitive Ben, and they shared a lot of quiet good times. But she can't forget Kemp—and it seems that he feels just the same.

Buy these books at your local bookstore or use this handy coupon for ordering:

within her grasp. It doesn't matter that Enid is Elizabeth's best friend—or that revealing the secret may cost Enid both her reputation and the boy she loves.

□ **#3 PLAYING WITH FIRE (On sale November 15, 1983 • 23972-4 • $2.25)**

Elizabeth doesn't trust Jessica's new boyfriend, Bruce Patman, one bit. He's arrogant, demanding—and way too fast. Jessica follows him everywhere, drops everything just to spend time with him. Jessica can usually hold her own with any guy, but this time Elizabeth's afraid Jessica may be going too far. . . .

□ **#4 POWER PLAY (On sale December 15, 1983 • 23730-6 • $2.25)**

Small, round Robin Wilson follows golden girl Jessica Wakefield around like a puppy. Jessica is everything that Robin isn't: beautiful, popular, and president of Pi Beta Alpha, the most exclusive and chic sorority at Sweet Valley High. Robin has her heart set on pledging—and to Jessica's complete astonishment, her own sister is determined to help!

Buy these books at your local bookstore or use this handy coupon for ordering: